# THE SUN ON MY HEAD

TRANSLATED FROM THE PORTUGUESE BY JULIA SANCHES

FARRAR, STRAUS AND GIROUX

NEW YORK

# THE SUN
# ON MY HEAD

STORIES

# GEOVANI MARTINS

Farrar, Straus and Giroux
120 Broadway, New York 10271

Printed in the United States of America
Originally published in 2018 by Companhia Das Letras, Brazil,
    as *O Sol Na Cabeça*
English translation published in the United States by Farrar, Straus and Giroux
First American edition, 2019

Library of Congress Cataloging-in-Publication Data
Names: Martins, Geovani, 1991– author. | Sanches, Julia, translator.
Title: The sun on my head : stories / Geovani Martins ; translated from the
    Portuguese by Julia Sanches.
Description: First American edition. | New York : Farrar, Straus and Giroux,
    2019. | "Originally published in 2018 by Companhia Das Letras, Brazil,
    as O Sol Na Cabeça."
Identifiers: LCCN 2018052637 | ISBN 9780374223779 (hardcover)
Subjects: LCSH: Rio de Janeiro (Brazil)—Fiction.
Classification: LCC PQ9698.423.A7556 A2 2019 | DDC 869.3/5—dc23
LC record available at https://lccn.loc.gov/2018052637

Designed by Jonathan D. Lippincott

Our books may be purchased in bulk for promotional, educational, or
business use. Please contact your local bookseller or the Macmillan Corporate
and Premium Sales Department at 1-800-221-7945, extension 5442, or by
e-mail at MacmillanSpecialMarkets@macmillan.com.

www.fsgbooks.com
www.twitter.com/fsgbooks • www.facebook.com/fsgbooks

10  9  8  7  6  5  4  3  2  1

*For Dona Neide, my mother.*
*For Érica, my partner.*
*And for all my brothers and sisters.*

# CONTENTS

# THE SUN ON MY HEAD

# LIL SPIN

FOR MATHEUS, ALAN, AND GLEISON

Woke up blowtorches blazing. For real, not even nine a.m. and my crib was like melting. Couldn't even see the rising damp in the living room, everything dry. Only the stains left: the saint, the gun, the dinosaur. Clear it was gonna be one of those days when you walking 'round and the sky's all fogged up, things shiftin' about like you hallucinating. Check it, even the breeze from the fan was hot, like the devil's fuggy breath.

My old lady had left two reals on the table for bread. Add to that another one-eighty and I could pay a one-way ticket at least, just had to sneak on dirty on the way out, when things chiller. Trouble was I'd turned the place upside down before hitting the sack, chasing coins for a loosey. Trick would be to sink the two reals into some bread, fix up a coffee, head to the beach with a full stomach. Fryin' at home just wasn't gonna fly. For kids like us, riding dirty's a cinch, the parley's slick.

Hit up Vitim at his place, then we rolled up to Cueball's and dropped in on Mish and Mash. So far everybody in the same boat: hard up, dopeless, wanting to chill beachside. But

Mash saved. Spent all night lending his buddies a hand with the package, so they threw him some bud. Crumbs left over from the kilo. Even got his hands on a capsule full of coke. Trouble was he wanted to bum around at home 'stead of coming with us. Mash's crazy. No way he gonna sleep under that star. Folks said on the beach he could just kick back, eyeball some babes, go for a dive to cool his dome. Be cruisin' by the time he got home, sleep like a baby. Mash said he'd throw a joint our way, but he was gonna chill at home, for real. Luckily, Vitim stirred him to snort a line to keep rumbling. Think that's all he wanted, a partner to blow with so he wouldn't roll alone, feelin' down. Those kids straight-up love that junk, never seen a thing like it. Ten a.m., the sun's slaying, and they stickin' their sniffers in snow.

Never done cola. I remember one day my brother came home from work lookin' all troubled, boladão, then called me to fire up with him in the back. Could tell straightaway he wanted to talk man-to-man. Reason for his bolação was a friend he grew up with had died, outta the blue. OD'd. He was on his bike, blasted outta his mind, prolly mission-bound, when he went down. Hit the ground stiff. Kid was my brother's age at the time, pô. Twenty-two! Never seen my bro like that, the two of them real tight. Then, he had words for me: best stick to weed. No coke, no crack, no pills, none of that shit. I should stay away from loló, too, 'cause that huff will melt your brain. And then there was all those kids who died of cardiac arrest 'cause they OD'd on that crap. That day, swore to him and to myself I'd never snort coke. Never mind crack, you crazy, that shit's lose-lose. Sometimes I'll do loló at a baile funk, but I take it easy. Now I see he was straight, you gotta stick to weed, even booze is junk. Get a load o' this, on my birthday I was crazy-wasted, clowning. Why? Cachaça! Worst thing is I can't remember nothin'. First, I'm boozin' at Mish and Mash's joint, playing cards, next thing I know I'm at home, filthy. 'Nother day, they lay it all on me. Said I been messing with some girls on the street, even followed a young piece down an alley. Talk of all kinds of dumb-ass clowning. Some fool catches me pullin' that and I'm sure to get my ass beat. Clap your eyes on that.

Driver didn't blink twice when our crew climbed in the back, bus was like full-up, with mad people, beach chairs, everybody sweaty, tight as tuna. Shit was grim. What got me through was just spacing, watching Mash and Vitim, the two fools bruxed outta their minds, chomping on their cheeks. Seriously, don't get why dudes do drugs just to get down on themselves, all paranoid 'bout everything. Like that time when Cueball and me was blazing on tia's terrace. Then Eightball sprouts outta nowhere with two paraíbas who'd just come down from their homeland. Shit, menó . . . The paraíbas went all out, snortin' one line after another, their eyes this wide, their teeth gnashin'. Then one of them bombed-out fools starts hearing sounds where there ain't none and we laughin' our asses off. Eightball, who's a joker, too, loosened his lips and started spinnin' that some cops was hiding on the next terrace over the way, ready to pounce. The paraíbas shat themselves in no time, flew off the terrace. Shit was rich! Fools dartin' about on the street, buggin' out, ducking behind walls, shit-scared the cops would sprout.

Real raid came 'bout a week later, that's when they took Jean from us, too. No joke, I don't even like to think on it, y'know, he was a good kid. All he wanted was to play his game, and boy was he a natural. Folks still saying to this day he coulda made it to the big leagues. Kid had a spot playing ball for Madureira, soon enough he'd be called to Flamengo or even a team like Botafogo. There, set! Seriously miss that son of a bitch, for real. Player was even playin' at his own funeral, four of his girls standing next to his ma, crying. Those police are all-out cowards, steppin' in on a holiday, guns blazin', folks out on the street, prime time to hit a kid. Should straight-up pump their blue asses full of slugs.

We hit the beach with the sun full-on blazin', babes sunnin' themselves, tails in the air, real chill. I dashed to the ocean, pulled some mad dives, cut through waves. Water was lush. Couldn't believe it when I came out and spotted the gang lookin' like they just stepped in shit. Trouble was some police in the area, scopin' us. Everybody ready to skin up, and there they be. Those beach cops are rough. Some days they lay the pressure on extra thick. To me, it's only one of two things: either they all smoke hounds itchin' to get high on other folks' weed, or they pushers wanting to sell grass to gringos and playboys, or hell knows. All I know's that when I see a cop break a sweat I get uneasy. Ain't good, for sure.

When motherfuckers finally cleared out, 'nother perrengue: nobody's got skins. Real drag, ain't it, menó? Bunch o' iron lungs and no skins in sight. Worst thing is we wasted all this time just on determinin' who'd go after the rags. Nobody wanting to ask the playboy potheads on the beach, all triflin', acting like they hot shit. When playboys on their own, they eye you kinda scared, like you schemin' to jump 'em. But when they with their buddies, they act like they the ones gonna come after you. Shit's foda, effed up.

Mish and Cueball tried their luck but came back empty-handed. These two kids nearby looked like they fierce into tokin'. Been showin' off ever since we hit the beach. Somebody comes by with Matte Leão, they buy it, with cookies, they buy it, açaí, they buy it, freeze pops, they buy it. Must of had some crazy-ass munchies. Already spotted a couple of boys eyein' them, waiting to strike. And fools just standing there, panguando, thinking they in Disneyland or some shit. Not to mention the dudes dressed as workers studyin' anybody with a bag, just waiting on the right time. That's what really gets me, shorty, menó. They just standing there, heads in the clouds. Then, when Mish and Cueball roll up to ask them something, all humble like, they get worked up, start shufflin' like they gotta guard their gear, glancin' about to see if any cops around. Bitch, please! Somebody really should mug these motherfuckers. Wasn't for my ma, I'd swipe all kinds of stuff off the blacktop, no joke, just outta spite. Trouble is my old lady's real uptight. Specially after what happened to my brother. She's always goin' on 'bout how if I end up in juvie at Padre Severino she'll never look me in the eyes again. Shit's wack.

If I hadn't stepped up, we woulda been screwed, for sure. Menós took another spin but no dice. Just some cheap napskins from a guy at the kiosk hopin' to blaze with us. Nobody wants to hear 'bout napskins no more, now it's all 'bout Smoking papers. Back in the day, folks used anything to smoke, notebook paper, bakery bags. Now it's all this fussy memeia. I hit the sidewalk and the jackpot: got my hands on a red skin. If you skillful in the roll, you can even cut a piece in half, make two blunts. Blew buddies' minds.

And it was dead easy, too, I just asked this rasta hawkin' reggae bracelets. Brother was solid, even threw me a cigarette. Told me to stay smart, that the pigs feelin' vicious these days. Somebody had popped a Bolivian in the sand, so the brass was comin' down hard on the beach, fearing more people might go down, 'haps even a local or a gringo, and then shit would fly, y'know? Making headlines and TV programs like *Balanço Geral*, that kinda chaos.

But the pigs out to lunch, ain't nobody dying here. Nah. Stuff was chill, the biz had been 'bout monies owed and now the fool who zeroed the Bolivian was takin' a break from the beach. Rasta said to stay on my toes if I was plannin' any tricks, but I said I was chill, just wanting to dig the beach, smoke my spliff on the down-low. He said I should never lose faith in God. Rasta was fly. Child of the Maranhão. Said weed up there's bountiful, everybody smokes, he started when he was ten, just like me.

After the blunt, I started trippin', watching seagulls flyin' on high. When I looked straight at the sun, everything glowed, way mellow, way marola. When I couldn't handle the heat no more, I doused my buzz in the water. That was the best part: catching crazy waves, just rockin', lettin' my body marola on the water till it dropped me in the sand. Then we all started battling to see who could stay underwater the longest. Mad perrengue: we all a bunch of smokers!

But steppin' outta the water, we peeped the wildest thing: playboys who nickel-and-dimed us on the skins was takin' selfies, acting like they divas or some shit. When they went to look, nothing left to see. Two young kids flew by, taking their backpacks with all their stuff, then ducked into the mobbed beach. Playboys stood there like bait, cells in hand, panguando. Then another kid rolls by and swipes their cells, too. That'll teach 'em not to be suckers. Laughed our asses off, the menós and me. Jokers split with only their sarongs in hand. Then I started thinking 'bout them hotfootin' shorties. They all hustlers, and the rasta said the beach was crawling with fuzz. I was rooting for them to dodge the pigs, you feel?

Next we know it's near dark and we got mad-ass munchies that, no joke, was like forty beggars and twenty Catholics all rolled up in one. Time to split. And that's when shit went nonlinear. We're walkin' all chill like, on our way to the bus stop, when we spot some cops coming down hard on a couple kids. Thing was they saw us, too, no time to even turn 'round and take another street. Up until then, menó, we didn't owe them nothing, crime was all in the mind, no fear. Just kept walkin'.

Just as we're passing the lineup with the kids facing the wall, sons of bitches tell us to roll up, too. Then they come out with this gab that if you got no money for a bus ticket you goin' downtown, you got way more money than a bus ticket, you goin' downtown, got no ID, you goin' downtown. Shit, my blood boiled double-time, no joke. I thought, I'm screwed; by the time I tell my old lady a pig's snout ain't no power outlet, she'll have beat my ass.

Didn't think twice. Ditched my flip-flops right then and there and scrammed. Cop yelled he was gonna get me. I felt sick, for real, just tore off, shitting myself, didn't even look back to see what was up. I thought of my brother and of us playing ball together on the street. He was always quicker than me, mad-fast. I was runnin' almost as fast as him, outta despair. Nearly cried with rage. I knew Luiz was no X9, that he'd never exnine on nobody. My bro died as bait, for nothin'. Instead of any one of those fools the world's full-up on. Always fills me with rage.

My body went head-to-toe cold, sure I'd been made. My

time had come. My old lady was gonna be left with no sons at all, all on her own in that house. I pictured Seu Tranca Rua, my grandma's protector, then Jesus, my aunts'. Don't know how I was managing to run, menó, for real, my whole body felt tight, everything stiff, you know? Everybody on the street lookin' at me. I turned my head to see if the pig was still on my ass, but he'd turned back to pat down those other boys. I was in the clear.

# SPIRAL

It started really early. I didn't understand. Once I began walking home from school on my own, I noticed this shifting. First with the kids from the private school on the corner of my school's street—they shook whenever my crew walked past. It was weird, funny even, because at our school my pals and I didn't scare anybody. Quite the opposite, we spent our lives running from bigger, stronger kids who were braver and more violent. As I walked around Gávea in my school uniform, I felt like one of those boys who bullied me in class. Especially when I passed in front of the private school, or when an old lady crossed the street, clutching her bag so she wouldn't bump into me. There were times, back then, when I enjoyed that feeling. But, as I said, I didn't understand a thing about what was going on.

People say that, compared to other favelas, in the North or West, or in the Baixada Fluminense, living in a favela in the South Zone is a privilege. In a way, I see why they'd think this, I guess it makes sense. What people don't often talk about is that in the South Zone, unlike in other favelas, the abyss that marks the border between the hill and the blacktop runs much deeper. It's rough walking out of those alleys, sharing the stairs with pipes upon pipes, stepping over open sewage drains, staring down rats, swerving your head to dodge electrical lines, and spotting your childhood friends carrying weapons of war only to be faced fifteen minutes later with a condominium with ornamental plants decorating its metal gates, and spying teenagers at their private tennis lessons. It's all too close and too far. And the more we grow, the taller the walls become.

I'll never forget my first chase. It all started in the way I hated the most: me, so distracted I was frightened by the person's fear and, next thing I knew, I was driving it, I was the threat. I caught my breath, my tears, stopped myself, more than once, from cursing out the old woman who was so obviously flustered about having to stand next to me, and only me, at that bus stop. But instead of moving away, as I always did, I inched closer. She'd try to look over her shoulder without seeming to watch me, I'd draw nearer. She started looking about her, searching for help, her eyes pleading, then I came right up next to her and looked directly at her purse, pretending to be interested in what it might hold, trying to seem capable of anything to get what I wanted. She walked away from the bus stop, her steps slow. I watched her drifting from me. I didn't quite understand what I was feeling. Then, without blinking, I started following the old woman. She soon noticed. She grew alert, stiff, her tension stretched to the limit. She tried to pick up her pace so that she could reach someplace, anyplace, as quickly as possible. But on that street it was like only the two of us existed. Now and then I'd pick up speed, savoring that fear, full of the dust of another time. Then, I'd slow down again, give her room to breathe. I don't know how long it all lasted, probably no more than a few minutes, but, to us, it had seemed like a lifetime. Until she stepped into a café and I kept on walking.

The whirlwind over, I felt disgusted for taking it so far, thinking of my grandma and of how this old woman probably had grandkids, too. But my guilt was short-lived. Soon, I remembered how that same old woman who'd trembled with fear before I'd given her reason to certainly hadn't given any thought to how I probably also had a grandma, a mother, family, friends, all those things that make our freedom worth much more than a purse, domestic or imported.

Even though it sometimes seemed crazy to me, I couldn't stop, because they wouldn't either. My victims were varied: men, women, teenagers, the elderly. Despite this diversity, there was always something that brought them together, as if they all belonged to the same family and were trying to protect a common patrimony.

Then came the loneliness. It became harder and harder to cope with any day-to-day things. I couldn't even focus on my books. I didn't care if it was raining or shining, whether Flamengo or Fluminense were playing on Sunday, if Carlos had split up with Jaque or there was a special promotion on at the movies. My friends didn't get it. I couldn't explain the reason for my absence, and so, little by little, I felt myself drifting away from the people who mattered to me most.

With time, this obsession started taking the form of research, a study on how humans relate to each other. I became both guinea pig and experimenter. I was beginning to

grasp my own actions clearly now, decode my instincts. Mean-
while, the difficulty I had in understanding my victims' reac-
tions seemed to grow by the day. These were people who
inhabited a world unknown to me. Not to mention that, since
I was supposed to be simultaneously acting, the time I had
to analyze my subjects face-to-face was brief and disorient-
ing. Realizing this, I reached the conclusion that I'd have to
target a single individual.

It wasn't at all easy finding this person. I became lost
among the many personalities, couldn't make up my mind.
I was frightened. Until one day, walking down the street late
at night, a man turned a corner at the exact moment I did, and
we collided. He raised his hands, surrendering to the assault. I
said: "Take it easy. And beat it." It'd been a long time since I'd
felt that same first, unfettered hatred, the kind that filled my
eyes with tears. For a while now, I'd abstracted myself from
those feelings of humiliation and even revenge. I'd been approaching my task from an ever more distant, scientific view-
point. But something in the way that man moved—the way
he raised his hands, the look of terror on his face—rekindled
the flame that had been lit the day I followed my first victim.
He was the one. It could only be him. I waited a moment and
then followed after him, invisible.

His name is Mário. I gathered this piece of information
from watching him closely as he greeted acquaintances on the
street near his place of work. He had two young daughters,
one around seven or eight years old, the other four, five at the
most. I didn't catch their names, because, whenever he was
with his family, I followed them from a distance, so as not to
raise suspicion. In the end, I christened the eldest daughter

Maria Eduarda and the youngest, Valentina. Names that suited their babyish, well-fed faces. His wife, I called Sophia. From where I stood, they seemed happy. On the day they went for a picnic at the Botanical Gardens, they played, ate cake, sweets, and looked at plants together. A bona fide butter commercial, with the exception of the nanny, who walked a short distance behind them, dressed entirely in white.

For the first month, I often orchestrated our encounters. During some of these, he felt intimidated by my presence, in others he appeared not to realize or care. I kept wondering when he'd register my existence. Three months. Until the day I saw in his eyes the horror of his realization. A lot changed after that moment. Mário became another person altogether. Always worried, looking over his shoulder. I watched. Sometimes I stalked him in plain sight, watching his tension grow until he was nearly bursting. Then I stopped, stepped into some establishment, acted natural.

Which brings us to the present. I spent a few days wandering the streets by his house. Once a privilege, living so close to work had become one of his greatest concerns. He'd try losing me by walking down different blocks, but his efforts were in vain; I'd known for a while where his apartment was located. Those were complicated days for both parties. I felt I was taking a definitive step forward but was unsure where this path would lead me. Until we arrived at the final round. I started stalking him, as usual, from a place close to his home. This time he didn't try to lose me, though. Instead, he took the fastest route back to his apartment. He sweated down the street, red-faced. I trembled at the thought of the many possible outcomes.

He entered his building, robotically greeted the doorman, went upstairs. A window. That's all I could see of his apartment from my line of sight. I fixed my eyes on that point, this time without hiding; if I saw him, he'd see me, too. A few minutes later, Mário appeared, a wild look in his eyes and an automatic pistol in his hand. I smiled at him, in that moment realizing that if I wanted to keep playing this game, I'd need a firearm, too.

# RUSSIAN ROULETTE

When he got to the street, they were all piled up in a circle, scrambling over each other. They paid no mind to the sun beating down on their heads and, instead of bickering over the scant shade under the acerola tree, fought for the best position from which to look at the porno photo comics that Oatmeal had found at home while rifling through his missing cousin's things. Paulo joined the gang, though he wasn't much interested in the magazine. It's not that he didn't like porn or quasi-porn, he was actually one of the boys who most lost his head when he saw women in bikinis getting all rubbed up in Gugu's pool over a bar of soap, or when he watched *Aventuras da Tiazinha*, in which a lingerie-clad heroine with a whip blows up bad guys, or by Feiticeira's dances on Luciano Huck's show. It's just that this time his world was turning differently.

"Damn. Check out blondie's tits. Look, look at the pussy on her. If I tapped a girl like that . . ."

"Outta the way, man. You got phimosis."

"Hell no I don't, show you my cock if you want."

"Whoa! Not only he got parachute-dick, he's a fag, too! Wants to show his dick to another guy!"

"What you on about, huh? Your sister can't even take a dump, that fatso's gonna blow any minute now!"

"Dude, I'm talkin' about you, you feel? About you, not your family. Motherfucker!"

"Mother what now? Say it again if you think you man enough!"

"Mother. Fuck. Er."

As he watched the scene unfold, Paulo had the impression he'd experienced moments like these before. He felt like he was seeing himself from a distance, anticipating every blast of sound on the street, every motion made by those piled-up bodies, every word that left their lips, even going so far as to anticipate that the coveted magazine would fall to the ground, abandoned in the face of the fascination the gun's presence had inspired in everyone.

It wasn't the first time Paulo played with his dad's gun. Every morning, as soon as he returns from the bathroom, he takes the iron out of the third drawer in the dresser under the TV. He likes to feel the gun's weight, to scrutinize its every component, to picture it in action. He can't quite make out how he feels about the adrenaline rush he gets from handling the weapon right in front of his dad, asleep on the bed beside him, whether it's good or bad. In that moment it's like all the air has suddenly been sucked out of the world, his whole body shivers, his heart races, his dad seems to shift and stir in slow motion, the slightest movement lasting an average of two to three lifetimes. The boy, unbreathing, weapon in hand. The man whose eyes might open at any moment. This is how their mornings go.

It was no secret there was a gun in the house. It would've been impossible, in that single room with a bathroom where they'd gone to live, to keep anything from the boy's prying eyes. When he accepted the job as a security guard and started carrying a .38, Almir decided to talk to Paulo. Man-to-man, he said, even though the boy had just turned ten. He said he needed the job, that it would make things better for the both of them, he'd make much more money than he did at the gas station. He said he trusted the boy with all his heart, which is why he didn't think twice before accepting the position and bringing the gun home.

Suspicious of relationships governed by fear, Almir often says he prefers to win his son over with respect. He repeats this to anyone and everyone, whenever he's asked about the challenges of raising a kid without a mother. In his attempt not to use physical force as the foundation of his son's education, he plays with the boy. He uses guilt and remorse to mold the kid's personality, his conscience light. For his part, Paulo doesn't know where respect, fear, shame, and the admiration he feels for his father begin or end.

For a while now, whenever Almir seems a bit more aloof in one of their father-son talks, Paulo wonders if he's figured out that he's been playing with his gun, if maybe he spotted him some morning, or if he realized that the drawer wasn't exactly as he'd left it. In these moments, cold sweat runs down his entire body and he wants to vanish forever.

Paulo often considers never touching the gun again, not causing a ruckus in the classroom anymore, or talking back to old folks on the street. All so as not to disappoint his dad. Only he knows what a pain Almir can be when he's disappointed. He always wants to talk for hours on end—about responsibility, and a bunch of other crap. Whenever he gets carried away by his words, Almir is like a preacher, and the feeling of being given a tongue-lashing is the boy's own personal hell. There are times when Paulo even thinks he'd be better off just getting smacked a half-dozen times and then sitting quietly in a corner, just like everyone else. But when it comes to living alone with his dad, the worst thing of all, the thing that makes the ground drop beneath his feet, is when his old man starts to cry. When that happens, he never knows what to do—if he should comfort him or pretend not to notice—and then he feels his face growing hotter, hotter until finally he also breaks into tears, often without understanding why. And so they both sit there, crying like a couple of bozos.

This time, Almir didn't head back to bed after lunch to sleep until his shift started. As soon as he finished smoking his palate cleanser, he went into the bathroom to get ready. And it had seemed weird to Paulo that his dad had showered before lunch instead of waiting until the usual time, since he only does so when he's about to go out. He never showers right after a meal, because it's bad for you, just like they say it's bad to mix mango with milk. Not just like, but worse. Because that's the kind of thing people die from.

The boy watched his father as he moved around the room. He put on his shoes, tidied his mustache, and buttoned his shirt, just like any other day, except this time he didn't take the gun. As Almir was about to walk out the door, Paulo felt the urge to warn his dad he was forgetting his weapon. Just then, he thought saying so might help raise him up in his dad's eyes; but on second thought, he was scared of seeming like he couldn't get the iron out of his head. He asked:

"Not going to work today, sir?"

"I'll be back in a bit."

As soon as he heard the gate to the vila close shut, Paulo ran to the door and locked it, leaving the key in the lock in such a way that it'd be impossible to open from the outside. Then he went to the drawer and reached for the gun. They were alone now for the first time.

The boy's imagination was soaring in the distance when it occurred to him that this might be another one of his dad's trust tests. The thought filled Paulo with remorse for all the crap he was always pulling, until he began to feel angry at himself. He couldn't understand why he had to be like that. Whenever his dad told him how he should behave, it seemed so easy. He'd fall asleep with the peace of knowing that tomorrow would be different. But next thing he knew, he was making the same mistakes, finding new ways to get into trouble. That swift and forceful wave of regret hit him just as he was feeling happy. And yet, the boy was so thrilled by the feat that he was soon able to pass through it, clinging to the certainty that never, not for anything in the world, would he be found out.

Everything was incredible, like in a dream, but it just wouldn't be enough, not unless he took the weapon out onto the street, not unless he showed it off to his pals. The trouble was that right then his friends were all holed up at home watching afternoon cartoons. Except for the kite junkies. There wasn't any point trying to show them anything, though, they never took their eyes off the sky, not even when the wind blew the kites so they were backlit by the sun.

The battle against the alien robots in the Japanese cartoon on TV just couldn't hold his attention. Throughout the episode, Paulo loaded and unloaded the gun again and again, pretending he was training for war. When he couldn't wait any longer, he pressed the iron's cool muzzle to his chest and dragged it down to his belly button, then pictured what it'd feel like to be shot right there, his entire stomach clenching at the image of the bullet piercing his flesh. He took the gun farther and farther down, until it reached his cock, and then moved it around in circles, savoring the hot-and-cold sensation of that encounter. Feeling himself go hard, he blushed with shame and quickly removed the .38 from his pants. Finally, he loaded it again while singing along with the TV to the cartoon's closing tune.

"They're blanks. The bullets."

"So? Blanks can kill, too. That's how Bruce Lee died."

"Huh, how?"

"He was making a movie and then they shot at him with blanks, 'cause that's what they do in movies, except he died. My uncle said he read it in a magazine. I think they shot him from real close."

◆

Paulo had to unload the gun before they could start playing cops and robbers. Everybody wanted to be on his team, which was a nice way to be. When his turn came to choose a side, he hesitated. Usually, Paulo liked to fight on the robbers' team, because chasing people all the time can be a real snooze. What he really enjoys is fleeing, making his body swerve, flaunting his agility, taunting his adversary. But this time he decided to side with the cops; he wanted to chase all of his friends down, every single one, to point the gun right at their heads, to press the trigger and use his mouth to simulate the sound of bullets breaching the barrel to chase after their destiny.

".38s are badass 'cause when the bullet goes in it makes a tiny hole, but when it comes out, it leaves a huge crater on the other side."

"You're crazy, man. What you're talking 'bout is a boomstick. I saw it in that movie *The Sixth Sense*, when that kid turns 'round and there's this gigantic hole in his head. In the back. That was from a 12-gauge, for sure."

"I watched that movie, too, you mope. Everybody did. That shot was from a Special. You wanna know more than I do, but my brother's in the army."

"Y'all can go on about Specials and boomsticks, but me, I'm all about the Golden Gun. A single shot anywhere, even your foot, you drop dead. Anyplace a bullet goes in, finds its way to the heart."

"My brother said those guns only exist in 007."

"And what does your brother know, punk? He's just a grunt."

It'd been a long time since they'd played cops and robbers. The craze at the moment was playing for stakes. Nine-ball, ringer, marbles, flipping for trading cards, tazos. What mattered was that it was worth something. Which is why chasing games, Paulo's favorite, were being left behind. Except during birthday parties on the street, 'cause on those days everybody wanted to run about and play all kinds of tag. Thinking back on those afternoon games, Paulo felt that's what life was really about, a party.

◆

"Y'all remember when that guy died right in front of Dona Margarida's place?"

"Yeah, I saw when the police rolled up."

"It's weird 'cause all they did was kill him. They left everything behind, the car, the money, everything. They were probably cleaning house."

"Yeah, that's what my aunt said, that they were cleaning house. She went to have a peek."

"What corpse does your aunt not peek at? My dad said she reads one of them if-it-bleeds-it-leads papers."

"Not anymore. She's scared that one day she'll open it and see a photo of my missing cousin."

All he wanted was for this to last forever. The awe in his friends' eyes, the attention he got no matter what he did. How awesome would it be if it were like this at school, too, he wondered. It's rough not standing out from the other boys in anything you do. Paulo wasn't the best at soccer, nor at playing marbles, nor flying kites. He wasn't one of the funniest or any good at brawling. Sometimes he felt that if he were to suddenly disappear, no one on his street or from his school would miss him. And yet, deep down he felt he had something very special inside, something unique that he couldn't reveal just yet, but that as soon as he did, everything would be different.

"I'm gonna tell you guys something, but it's a secret. My dad killed somebody with that gun."

"Quit telling tales, man, your dad's real chill."

"Sure, he's chill, until somebody messes with him. Just like me!"

"And how do you know this, huh, did you see it, did he tell you?"

"I heard him talking 'bout it with a friend, it was really early in the morning, and I was pretending to sleep so I could

listen to them talk. They were both nervous as hell. I remember there were other guns on the table, too."

"You were dreaming, man."

"Oh, look, the guys are putting the goalposts away. Let's
see if we can use them for a quick match."

Paulo was knocked back by that information. For the
older kids to be calling off the match it had to mean it was
getting dark and they were on their way home to shower so
that, later, they could hang out by the gates to their girlfriends'
houses, which meant it was almost around the time his dad
left work. He hightailed it out of there, without a care to what
his friends might think. He was filled with such despair he
couldn't even cook up a defense strategy, like he usually did
whenever he was heading home knowing he'd messed up.
And, to make his anxiety worse, on his way back he was as-
saulted by the sad certainty that it was all just a trap laid out
by his dad to see if he could trust him. He hated the fact that
he'd been so dumb, and he felt sorry for his pops, too, for having a son like him. Though as he approached their house, his
feelings seesawed—at times he felt he hated his dad, then he
felt sorry for himself—but this spinning wheel of emotions
didn't matter; it was all a steaming pile of shit no matter how
you sliced it.

He spotted his old man's shoes at the door as soon as he
walked through the vila gate and picked up the smell of his
cigarettes. He was sure he was done for. He couldn't imagine
what his life would be like after that day. He walked in, trying
not to make a sound, as if such care could save him from
finding his dad inside the room. He trembled just picturing
how he would look, sitting on the bed, wanting to talk about

what had happened. If there was a talk at all; he knew he'd gone too far this time. Luckily, when he finally got up the courage to walk through the door, he saw that the shower was on and Almir was beneath a stream of water. Paulo immediately put the gun back in the drawer and sat down to await whatever came next. This time, he was the one whose eyes filled with water. He clenched his fists to drive away an oncoming sob, said to himself "I'm a man," and decided that as soon as his dad came out of the bathroom, he'd confess to everything, before he even had the chance to ask any questions.

Some more time passed, and during this time, he remained certain that his best option was to make the first move. But the shower ran on, opening up room for so many more possibilities. If this time he got off scot-free, he'd never behave like that again, he swore this with the same truthfulness as he had in the past. He really wished the world would end before the shower did, but it didn't. Paulo heard Almir turn off the sounds of the drizzling water, rub the towel over his body, clonk his Prestobarba down on the sink, and then, finally, open the door.

# THE CASE OF THE BUTTERFLY

"Nobody's born a butterfly," Breno thought. Then he whispered: "A butterfly is a gift from time." Out there, she, the butterfly, didn't think this. She was busy fluttering through the night from tree to tree. She was blue and without a doubt had once been a caterpillar. Breno was nine years old and a kid. The caterpillar was like a kid-butterfly. Except when Breno grew up he'd be a man, not a butterfly, and men didn't fly. Breno dreamed of flying, as a pilot or a soccer player. As a butterfly, well, that was something Breno had never considered. He may have been nine, but he knew he was a boy, not a caterpillar. Breno's grandma was always saying: "Caterpillars munch on plants and burn your little fingers, but they grow up to be butterflies. Nobody's born a butterfly." Now the boy thought, as he watched the butterfly on the window, "This morning, I saw a bunch of little holes on the leaves." Someone had once explained to him: "It's those caterpillars." The holes in the acerolas and guavas were because of those birds. But no one had had to explain this to him, because he was always seeing the birds pecking at fruit, except for hummingbirds, who were always lapping at the water in the flower-cup that hung off the guava tree. "I wonder what caterpillars eat. Do hummingbirds only drink water?" He contemplated this at length and then felt hungry. He walked to the kitchen.

His grandma was napping in front of the seven o'clock telenovela. The one she most liked napping through. Breno knew this and didn't want to wake her to ask for food. The kitchen window was open. It was an enormous window that looked out onto their backyard. Breno had sometimes heard people talking about how funny that kitchen window was. His grandma would explain that before being a kitchen, it had been a room, which was why it had a window. Breno thought it was normal. Ever since he could remember, this had been the kitchen and the kitchen had a window and he loved it very much. While his grandma made lunch, he looked out at the world. People who didn't have windows were the unlucky ones.

Breno decided the best thing to eat right then was a cookie. "I hope we've got some. If not, I want eggs." He knew how to cook them: all he had to do was light the flame by pressing the button, place the frying pan over the flame, break the egg on the frying pan, and keep scrambling it with a fork. Now that he was nine he didn't need a chair to reach the stove anymore. He opened the fridge and there were three eggs. He closed the fridge and went off in search of a cookie. A butter-fly flitted into the kitchen. It was bigger and prettier than the last one. She seemed desperate, knocking into one wall after another until she became trapped by the closed door. Breno went to the door and opened it so she could leave, and she flew from that end to the other end of the kitchen, where the stove and window were. Breno followed her with his eyes and hoped she'd be able to fly out through the window. An uncovered pan filled with oil (they'd had fries for lunch) sat on the stovetop, the butterfly flitted toward the stove and, just as she was hovering above the pan, plopped into the oil as if it were pulling her in, just like when Breno would pull coins with his magnet.

He ran to see the butterfly, slowly swimming through the oil. He wanted to take her out but had never put his hand in oil before. It only burned when the flame was on, he was almost sure of it. He ran to the paper towel roll, then plucked the butterfly from inside the pan. He looked at her carefully, all covered in oil. Every single part of her insect body. As he walked, her wings dripped oil across the kitchen. He was certain now: it only burned when the flame was on. The butterfly fluttered about a lot. He tried to set her on top of the window.

He took the cookie and walked to his room. He started eating. The cookie was chocolate and yummy. But he couldn't stop thinking about the butterfly swimming in the oil. Her entire body submerged in it. He soon started picturing what it would feel like if he were the one dunked in oil in a gigantic pot big enough to hold children. He pictured his hair drenched in oil, his eyes, ears, mouth, nose. Eating his cookie, he imagined. He licked the finger he'd stuck in the pan so he could better picture his body in the oil. He didn't like picturing this, but he couldn't help it. It was like when you go and sniff your smelly hand, or something like that. He licked it and it tasted yucky. Much worse than a chocolate cookie. He remembered his grandma saying that if you get butterfly dust in your eye you'll go blind. He was scared he'd get sick. Besides oil, the finger he'd just licked probably had some of that dust on it, too. He ran to the kitchen to look at the butterfly. She was stiff, dead. He felt sorry for her, wanted to bury her. He decided butterflies would be his favorite animal—if he didn't get sick from licking his finger. He would have to tell his grandma not to fry any more potatoes in that pan. He would leave the butterfly on the kitchen window, while the sun was still down. On his way back to his room, he saw that his grandma was still napping. He got into bed and dipped his head in the oil for the last couple of times. He didn't want to get sick from the butterfly dust, it was all he could think of. Nobody's born a butterfly. The boy felt fear and something or other in his tummy, was frightened by the thought that the feeling was from the dust that blinds you when it gets in your eyes, and then fell asleep.

# THE TALE OF PARAKEET AND APE

When the UPP invaded the hill, buying any kinda shit was rough. The spot was sketch; no one wanting to show their faces to sling, nobody but kids pushing drugs. Eight-, nine-year-old shorties. Times I even felt sorry for those kids, seeing them like that. Thing is, we get used to all kinds of dark shit, and sorry's a feeling you get and lose quick; folks kept on buying drugs.

Best thing you ever did, meu mano, my dude, was head up to Ceará back then, straight up. Shit got wild, with cops comin' down hard, breaking into houses, chewin' out locals for any old crap. You know what they like. Specially with the papers closin' in on them, you had to see it. Dudes find a gun, half a dozen walkie-talkies and bam, it's front-page news, with fools thinking they gonna put an end to this trade. You gotta be real fucking thick. Go on, ask how many rifles they found, how many fat packages, how many big-cheese thugs they locked up. Blows my mind whenever I go out for a spin on the blacktop and realize nobody knows what's goin' on up here.

Not long till shit went sideways. Parás settling their troubles with blades, junkies swiping bars, locals, fools even broke into Ricardo Eletro. When hoods holed up so cops could roll in, shit was like no-man's-land, menó. On top of that, hill's top dogs had all split to other, chiller favelas. Us locals the ones who got screwed, as usual. Cops always stoppin' us on the street asking where we goin', what we doin'. Tell me, goddamn, motherfuckin' bullshit, we born and raised in this crap just to keep pleasing the brass? Everybody already brimming with hate.

Soon as trade kicked up again, guns were dug up, folks got put to work, and pushers and lookouts scattered for real, so they could get back to making dough. It was rough goin' in the early days, with slugs flying steady. Been years since so many shots fired in Rocinha. Almost an everyday kinda thing, you'd wake up in the morning just waiting on the salvo to sing. At first, it was just to scare the cops, show them nobody jokin' 'round here. But before long folks started dropping on both sides.

After a while, fools got tired of being at it 24/7, and each kept to their own corners. Cops on one side, hoods on the other, shit started going back to normal. Could even fire up on the street—on the down-low, but you could. What blew was the bud seemed to be getting worse by the day. Get this: couple days after the UPP rolled in, you could buy stuff again, but by then it's a different kind of bud. Never got that shit. Remember benga, was that slung back in your day? Right, well, y'know how it was dead stale but still fried your dome? I remember like it was yesterday, mano, last day before the police crept up the hill. Vibe was real tense, nobody sure what might go down. One gang thought no way players gonna hand over the hill, that they'd shoot till they couldn't, then wait for it to make news so the governor would put a stop to it all. Word was the hill was huge, that folks could fan out and keep the pigs from comin' in. Shootin' had to stop at some point, though, on account of the locals. Another gang thought they'd hand the hill over quick, then take it back, no point in them just firin' at each other, they'd call in the military for sure, just like they did in Alemão. But nobody knew nothing for certain, that's what's rough. Worst part's always picturing shit you know will go down but don't know how. Right, so that day, the day before they invaded, I went to buy a joint on Via Ápia 'cause at the time I was living in a small room on Travessa Kátia; rolling in, I peeped Renatim, a buddy from back in the day who'd gone to school with me and shit. Didn't even know he was back in the boca, dealing. Last time we met he was working at a drugstore in São Conrado 'cause he had a baby girl on the way. In the boca, folks acting like stuff was chill, but you could tell something was off. I'm telling you all this 'cause I remember I bought some benga there then—that was the last time. After the cops came in, they started sellin' that old, dry, stepped-on junk we're all smoking now.

Just as folks thinking the worst had come and gone, Ape Face comes into the picture. A son-of-a-bitch lieutenant who rolled up looking for a fight. What really hacked me off was brasshead didn't give a crap about catching any drug traffickers. His beef was with junkies. Said traffickers only exist 'cause junkies do. Fucking hell, menó, blows my mind. I was back in Cachopa back then, and that was his beat. He blew in savage every day, always at a different time; if he caught anybody smoking or snorting, or if he got it into his dome some fool was on his way to buy drugs, he chewed them out hard. Motherfucker had no mercy, straight up, made the first junkie he caught sniffin' snow in the boca snort the entire eight-ball right in front of him, all in one blow. At one p.m., the sun blistering. Then he started banging coker's head against the wall, fool's face got all mashed up.

Another time, now this was fucked up, Ape Face drove Neguinho into the ditch. Kid was smokin' grass on the slope up to Vila Verde when he peeped the cops coming at him and threw his joint in the ditch. What for, menó. Ape Face went savage on him. Shoved his gun in the kid's face, asked where he got hold of the bud. Neguinho said he bought it at Parque União, that folks was buying stuff down that way 'cause the hill was dry. Ape Face pistol-whipped Neguinho on the dome, and stoner went down on the double. Ape Face asked him again, said he'd put a bullet in his head if he didn't spill, or he could go and throw himself in the ditch. Neguinho didn't think twice and jumped. Now folks say he's got lectospirosis, that bug that's in rat piss.

But shit started for real when Ape Face got his hands on a playboy coming down Cachopa slope. Player was carrying weed, cola, pills, lança-perfume, and all that junk in his pack. Sushi'd brought him over for his monthly run. Ape Face started railing on the playboy right there on Estrada da Gávea, in front of everybody. Said that then he goes and gets himself shot, and there's no use complaining 'cause he's the one giving money to the guys buying guns. These po-po are a fucking joke, for real, when they spout that kinda crap, almost makes it seem like they ain't the ones selling the motherfucking guns on the hills. But there's a twist to the story. See, playboy didn't wimp out, nah, instead he started arguing with the brasshead, rising and rising. Pretty soon, Ape Face starts backpedaling. Player just had to be connected to pull a stunt like that. And he was, kid's daddy was a big-shot judge or somethin', one of them heavyweights who make cops crap their pants.

Ape Face went straight-up apeshit. Word is he cleared outta there frothing at the mouth like a dog and rolled up the slope hungering to harm. Lookouts clocked and scrammed, dropping warnings to folks on the street. That's when Ape Face spotted Buiú toking up on the terrace with Limão. Except, like, back then a bunch o' cops had sent word that if we were gonna smoke grass, we gotta do it on the terraces. Specially since they don't even know how to get up there, so it's always been the quietest part of the hood. Ape Face hid 'round there till shorties climbed down. Then, he pussyfooted up to the two boys and rung 'em. But he ain't done nothing out on the street, not like other times. Instead, he took the kids up to Mestre's joint, that was already their base back then, and started wailin' on them. Word was he thrashed the shorties all night long. Folks say they even shoved a carrot up the boys' butts, some real trifling shit.

What Ape Face didn't know was that Buiú was like a blood brother to Pistol Parakeet. And you know, right, Pistol's batshit, no joke. Specially if you take into account that for a brother who talks soft—even if it's 'cause of a throat thing—only way to get respect in the boca is to be boss in a shoot-out. Fool made a name for himself back when bullets flew steady, came to be the kingpin's right hand and stuff. So, Parakeet, who was already hating on those Cachopa cops, flipped his shit after that Buiú nonsense. Went on and on 'bout how he was gonna avenge his brother. At first, folks thought he was saying all that crap 'cause he had to, that it

would stop there. After a while, though, people started be-
lieving he was for real, even tried to get him to give up on
that bunk, to let it go, that there'd be trouble for everybody if
he killed that pig.

No stoppin' him, though. No brother who's a man lets a
fool mess with his family. I feel him on that. Trouble was Ape
Face always made his rounds with four, five other brassheads,
and pumpin' lead on your lonesome against a whole crew just
won't cut it, it don't fly. Parakeet wasn't even sleeping no more.
He burned through night after night snorting dust and
plotting revenge, till the day finally came when his mind
cleared and he struck gold.

What he needed to get the plan rolling was a hot young
thing, and, all modesty aside, that's something we got no short-
age of in Cachopa. She couldn't just be fine, though, she had
to be freaky, too, a shrewd-ass cookie. That's when he thought
of Vanessa. How come? First of all 'cause she's fine as hell,
second 'cause she'd been turning tricks for a while now, so
she had the chops and the cool to do shit the way he wanted
it done.

Plan was for her to take Ape Face to a shack Parakeet had
rented just for the purpose. Dead easy. Vanessa called him
aside, like she was an X9, saying she's got something important to share. So he went, right, who wouldn't? She says to
him that men in uniform get her all hot and bothered, that
she keeps on dreaming of him and waking up all wet,
speakin' in the kind of voice that gets any fool hard in a hot
minute. The other cops wanted to go with him, thinkin'
they'd have a bacchanal, but she said her want was with him
only, and Ape Face liked that—fool must of never boned a girl

like her without paying—and that's when he sends all them other bums back to the base.

Parakeet was waiting inside the bathroom for Ape Face, an M16 zeroed at the door. Plan was for Vanessa to step into the bathroom and then, if everything seemed cool, send Ape Face in to face the bulletstorm. But, soon as they stepped into the shack, brasshead started pulling Vanessa's clothes off and, being no fool, she let him, even pretended to like it. She got his vest off, his uniform, then both of them ended up naked in bed. She tried to get up and go to the bathroom, but he wouldn't let her. That's when she started moaning real loud, so Parakeet could hear her for real in there. He crept out on the sly, and by the time Ape Face clocked, the muzzle was kissing him. Vanessa shook loose from the pig and spat on that ape-faced motherfucker.

Couple kids helped Parakeet carry the body into the bush where he set the cop ablaze. Then he hotfooted off the hill. He'd been warned shit would fly if he killed the dude, and shit did. Raid after raid followed on account of that business. But after a month or so, everything was easy again 'round Cachopa.

After they couldn't find Ape Face's body no way, they printed a picture of him in the paper that said: "Lieutenant Roberto de Souza's children cry at their father's symbolic burial." For real, even I—and I hate them cops—felt a bit sorry in that moment, seeing those kids like that.

# BATHROOM BLONDE

When the school year ended, André wouldn't even let his classmates sign his shirt. It was his last day there and he was fed up with the place, the teacher, the students, everything. On top of that, every time a hottie asked him where he went to school and he had to say Antônio Austregésilo, he died of embarrassment. "Shit," he'd think, "is that any kinda name for a school or, worse, a person?" Even so, when it came to names, he was comforted by the fact that some of his friends went to much-worse-sounding places that, said aloud, invited immediate ribbing, leading to refrains such as: "Ubaldo de Oliveira, entra burro e sai caveira," go in a dummy, come out a mummy. Or the classic: "Djalma Maranhão, entra burro e sai ladrão," go in a deadbeat, come out a cheat. At least Austregésilo didn't rhyme with anything, it just had the rotten luck of being real ugly. On top of all that, there was the fact that André was a repeater in a primary school—in other words, in a school full of seven- and eight-year-olds. Soon enough, he'd be twelve, basically a teenager.

Everything would change once he was at Henrique.

André was sure of it, certain he'd lucked out. Knowing everybody respected his future school 'cause the kids there were badass, he dreamed of being badass, too, and taking advantage of the weekly bouts against the Getúlio crew to make a name for himself. Around there, the only school that clashed head-on with Getúlio in a punch-up was Henrique. Their quarrel was part of a rivalry passed down through generations—one whose beginning no one could explain and its end much less predict—a conflict that held a series of thrilling tales that were performed at no set time on the streets of Bangu.

André was always spacing out. In class, at mass, during family lunches. He was always someplace else, fantasizing about everything with the same passion and the same sense of urgency. Only on vacation did he feel he didn't have to day-dream. He preferred to keep his feet planted on the ground, to run lightning-fast, to feel the loud beating of his heart. Except, this time, he couldn't stop picturing his debut at the new school. Even with kites, marbles, and spinning tops rolling during the day, and friendly soccer matches bringing every-body together at nightfall, he'd always find a little nook in his thoughts in which to dream of the not-too-distant future.

On the eve of his first day of school, he didn't sleep a wink. He spent the entire night rolling about on the sofa bed, picturing his new life at the big kids' school. He'd have eight teachers now, one for each course. He could fail up to two subjects and then make them up the following year. He'd made up his mind to join in on the first brawl to defend his school, and he'd fight with so much team spirit he'd fall into favor with the older kids. Not that he liked tussling or was particularly skillful at kicking and punching—until then he'd shown himself to be second-rate in fights against kids his age—but there was no getting around it, he was certain that this was the only way he could gain the respect he needed. Otherwise, his life would be hell: head-smacked and teased for being a shrimp, from Monday to Friday until he reached seventh grade.

He left behind his colored pencils, ruler, pens, and everything else in the list of materials off which his mom had made a point of buying every single item—no matter how much it hurt her pocket—and instead took only his Flamengo notebook and a Bic pen. Sitting in the front row with a pencil case and answering the teacher's questions were all terrible ideas for anyone who intends to be respected at school.

Through the circular holes in the wall that served as windows, he could see the soccer pitch. It was big, with a covering and everything, and even a changing room where you could shower after PE. Although he was nervous, trying to control each step he took, André still found it in him to savor a bit of every novelty.

He spotted two girls sitting at the other end of the pitch, near the metal fence, smoking a cigarette out of sight from the monitor. Watching that scene, he felt content, seeing himself in that moment as the girls' accomplice. He felt he was growing up, maturing in the face of this new life unfolding before him. What would he be doing when he turned twenty? Would he be a businessman, a soccer player, a parachutist?

The last period before recess was French, and André didn't understand a thing. He couldn't stop staring at the teacher's unibrow and, also, wasn't the least bit interested in the language. What he really wanted was to learn English, 'cause everybody says it makes you rich, and also because of video games. He was sure that if he knew the language spoken by the characters in people's favorite video games, everybody'd invite him over to play with them. At the time, learning English in school was an easier challenge than getting his own console from his mom. He only snapped out of it once the bell rang, hearing a schoolmate inform the class that in French *cou*, which sounded like "ass" in Portuguese, actually meant "neck." Once he absorbed this piece of information, he started warming to the class. The language might not be useful, André thought, but it sure was funny.

The eighth-graders stood at the door to the cafeteria. André spotted them as soon as he reached the patio. He knew that to survive a place like that he'd have to be strong in the face of any kind of terror. "There's no lunch today," they said. André looked at every one of their faces, trying to make the toughest possible expression, to seem dangerous and unpredictable. "Everybody in the can, now," said one of the kids, who looked like a playboy with his straightened, bleach-blond hair. And everybody went. Once they were all inside, the boys spelled out how things worked in the school. André pored over every word. It seemed fair. "Every newbie gotta pass this test," they said after explaining the rules. André immediately thought it'd be something pedophilic. He hadn't prepared himself for that, hadn't imagined that in the big kids' school, where girls smoke and have sex, he'd have to go through that kind of thing. But that wasn't it.

It was the Bathroom Blonde test. André knew that story inside out and couldn't believe that's what they were doing. Bathroom Blonde was a girl who'd killed herself after being raped in the school bathroom. Ever since then, every time someone said "Bathroom Blonde" in front of the mirror, she'd appear. Then, you had to run away as quickly as possible, before her spirit took over the bathroom, 'cause if you were still there when she showed up, there were only two options: either the girl's presence drove you crazy or you were abducted into the mirror.

André had challenged her once on his own, out of sheer curiosity, and managed to get away. But he'd felt so scared he promised himself he'd never, not for anything in the world, do it again. He said to the kids:

"C'mon, give us a real test, pô. All that talk about the Bathroom Blonde is just to scare the little kids at Antônio." He chuckled half-heartedly.

Then the kid with the straightened hair announced: "Seein' as you don't believe, you'll go first. Everybody outta the bathroom."

Everyone left, the door closed, the lights went out. André was burning up thinking of the head-smackings he'd take, the hotties he wouldn't tap, the soccer matches he'd miss, and all the awful things that would happen if he faltered in that moment. He steadied his wobbling legs, took a long breath, looked deep into the mirror's eyes and spoke the words: "Bathroom Blonde, Bathroom Blonde, Bathroom Blonde."

# THE TAG

He wasn't supposed to be there. Suddenly, everything became muddled: he was drinking beer, filled with nostalgia, pride, want. A kid rocked up with some spray, word on a spot he'd scoped, the metal ball dancing in the can, the sharp smell of adrenaline. Next thing he knew, he was on his way up to the building's rooftop terrace, scared off by the woman's terrified screams: "Thief! Catch him!"

The kid with the spray paint was just another one of those boys who spent their lives paying homage to graffiti kings, xarpi big shots: wanting to throw them cigarettes, brew, bud, and, of course, spray. All in the hopes of someday setting off on a mission together, their names tagged side by side on the same gazebo, eaves, window. Or even on a tintão, pebble-dash wall, gate. What mattered was sticking together, slurping up fame like a blood-sucking tick. The world was fed up with these kids, so was Fernando.

I say Fernando because by then he'd dropped the name he'd used to tattoo the city. It was coming up on three months since he'd left xarpi behind, he wasn't dropping marker tags

anymore and even avoided tracing the motion of the letters
with his fingers. On the bus, he'd try and find other dis-
tractions to keep himself from looking out the window: he
read books, the paper, messed about on his phone, followed
the horoscopes flashing on ad screens. He was recalibrating
his relationship to the city so he wouldn't become so pumped
about scoping out heavens, tripping over the legion of legit
names that crossed his path.

After his son, Raul, was born, Fernando did what he
could to change course. It's rough, fighting your instincts. He
didn't want to want to hit x peak in x place, didn't want to
be recognized at meets as Maluco Disposição, for being a fool
who's always game, or be called to sign with initials that, by
then, were relics. What he really wanted was to look after his
kid, to stay alive, be present. But he always knew that to do so,
he'd have to leave xarpi behind, to let the persona he'd erected
on a wing and a prayer die. Or, at least, to take fewer risks,
throw stuff up on the down-low, go on easier missions.
Which, at the end of the day, is a much worse kind of death.

He didn't catch where the shots came from, couldn't
tell if it was the police, militia, or locals. It didn't matter; on
the blacktop at daybreak, it's always you against the world.
Luckily, the building was low, only five stories high, and he'd
nearly reached the top by the time the woman started yelling
and the chaos broke. Good thing his reflexes were top-notch:
he reached the terrace in a split second, caught his breath.
From way up high, he hunted the spray kid with his eyes, but
the son of a bitch had ghosted, hadn't even made it up the
building.

He considered tossing the spray can, explaining that he
wasn't a thief and wasn't there to take anything from anybody.

It was just the opposite: he wanted to leave his mark on that tile wall, a gift. He already knew everything he was gonna do: the size of the sequence of names, the spacing between one name and the next. He'd even throw in a line by the Racionais, "Pesadelo do sistema não tem medo da morte"— the system's nightmare fears no death—and dedicate it to those friends who'd given their lives for art.

In the end, he didn't toss the can. In the minds of those who wear the cape of justice in this sort of situation, taggers and thieves nearly always have the same worth and the same destiny. Fernando was aware of all that, he knew his rivals well, the result of years challenging them on the street. He didn't resent them, he knew they were essential to the game. After all, street tagging wouldn't make much sense without all those people who were willing to do anything to keep those names and colors from spreading across properties and streets. You can only play with both teams on the field. He decided to wait, to temper the game. If they didn't spot anybody soon, they'd split. This time, he wouldn't win, the wall would remain clear of his marks, and yet he believed strongly that, sometimes, a draw was a good outcome.

Tags are about eternity, about marking your passage through life. Fernando, like most people, felt he couldn't go through this world unnoticed. Next thing he knew, he was hanging around all the taggers on his block. It was wild hearing stories of names that had lived on in that city for over twenty, thirty years, and that would surely—even after they were scrubbed out and their walls knocked down—live on in people's memories. That's how he wanted to make history, remembered and respected by the right people. And this had always been his greatest motivation at the moment of tagging—more than fame, dissent, or aesthetics, though they all conspired for it to make sense. What he really wanted was to mark his city and his time, to traverse generations on the street, to become visual.

But his son's arrival had made a mess of his ideas. The boy was a second chance at life, right there in his arms. He had his features, soon he'd have his smile, his way of talking. But if this is what Fernando wanted, he couldn't be there in that building. When he announced he was planning to quit, everybody started giving him lip, saying dude hadn't quit for his ma, now he's gonna go and quit for his girl. And as much as it nagged him to be pegged as pussy-whipped, Fernando didn't even bother talking back.

Some days the sun shines even after dark, the heat and sweat-drenched bed don't let anybody sleep right, and people go outside needing fresh air, which is why the crowd way down there kept growing, even past two a.m. They arrive not knowing what's going, are told the reason for the gathering, and become enveloped by the street and by its incredible capacity to transform common folk—who love and cry, feel hunger, nostalgia—into something altogether different, a unit that extends beyond the confines of each of the individuals gathered and is unflustered by the sight of blood running down the clothes of the affected target, should it, at the exact moment of the blow, satisfy their sense of justice. Once again a thirst for justice to be served against the unknown, just as it had always been, since the beginning of time. Fernando looked down at the crowd with surprise. There's danger in the tag, mankind's rotten, that much he's always known. For every action there's a reaction, and everybody's got to face their own music.

What he wanted was to put himself out there and tag that entire building, in front of everybody. To show them that, even after paint hit property, life went on. Until a higher power—such as God or a gun—decided to put a stop to it.

He tried but couldn't make out the exact moment he'd let himself go, when one force had overcome another until he'd found himself there. He had the sense that life never left room for making plans, things kept happening, one way or another, trampling over any projects in their way. Only in the future—when it arrived—could we understand, and laugh or cry, at the stories we'd lived.

Fernando remembered his dad banging on the door. A stiff sound. His mom would say: "No one open that!" She only ever let him in when he was sober and was well-acquainted with the sounds of his drunk bashing. She'd spent a pretty penny on all those locks, but at least her kids wouldn't have to see their dad passed out on the kitchen floor. Fernando would feel like opening the door, remembering the times his old man had taught him to fly kites and taken him to the fair in Quinta da Boa Vista, or when they'd made paper balloons together to let loose on holy days.

He had a bad feeling. For the first time since the night had begun, he felt things slipping out of his control. It wasn't long before his body was seized by despair. Something amid all the things that were happening warned him that, this time, he wouldn't get off lightly. It wasn't at all like a movie flashing life before death, as they say, but a living memory, messy, reeling backward and forward the entire time, thumping in free fall over the utter uncertainty, pounding at the same speed and with the same force as his heart. It was pain, fear, and a hatred of life, all together, mixed up with the building, the shots, his son, the screaming woman, all those people down there.

This time, the adrenaline worked against him. It shouted the same mantra as always, that we only live once, but with the opposite effect. Instead of stoking his courage, it smothered him. Smothered like a body, any body overcome by fear.

While he was clean of xarpi, Fernando liked to come home early, dashing out of work and into his wife's arms, to his son's still-toothless smile. Sometimes, he'd buy some food for them on the street, on weekends they drank wine or beer, depending on the weather. He liked it when, lying in bed, instead of thinking of spots to tag on the blacktop, he thought only of how lucky he was to be alive.

From up high on that building, looking down at the impromptu patrol, Fernando couldn't help himself, he thought of his dad. Of how, once he'd quit trying to get through that door, he'd bounced from one relative's house to another till he found himself almost definitively on the street, sinking nearly his entire retirement into cachaça. Fernando remembered the times he said he'd be better to his son than his dad had been to him, that he'd give Raul everything he'd been without. In that moment, feeling the burden of his choices, he had the strength to remove himself a little from the place he'd always been. A pity he was dead, his dad, and that the urge he felt to apologize was in vain.

Things couldn't stay the way they were. He had to fix the situation, take control, study the possibilities. Had the crowd down there spotted him? He didn't think so, didn't want to believe it, but would they really spend so much time looking for someone with no leads? Better to accept it, they'd seen him. And they were waiting. That must be it.

In that case, there was no other way but to parley his way out. If he stayed quiet, he could very well take a bullet as he tried to flee; out of fear, you never know. He ditched the spray can, waited a few seconds until he heard the clang confirming his message had been delivered, then yelled "I'm a tagger!" and felt alive.

After that first attempt at a conversation, one of the residents opened the door to the building and let the men up. A handful stayed down there, eyes peeled for a possible escape. It was clear they didn't want to talk. Fernando knew that by staying where he was, he wasn't in danger of being shot close-range. Not with so many people following events, and inside a residential building. He'd almost certainly be dealt a nice beating, though—the delay and who knows how many other frustrations taken out on him with kicks and punches.

Trouble is, beatings can kill, too. He'd never forget all the friends he'd lost, pummeled on the blacktop, suffering cranial trauma and internal hemorrhaging. And, even if his time hadn't come, if he survived the thrashing, at home he'd still have to explain how he'd gotten all those hematomas, and they'd know he was tagging again, that he'd given in to his addiction, and he'd be accused of being weak, a hypocrite, of constantly moaning about how his dad had chosen the bottle over him and now, there he was, choosing spray over his own son.

The weight of his body broke the roof of the next building, the noise taking everyone by surprise, slicing through the silence and static tension that had gripped the night until that moment. Luckily, the ground wasn't far, the roof was over the building's depot, where they stored all kinds of junk. The perfect hiding place, he thought. Only then did his foot start hurting, like hell, as if he'd twisted or, worse yet, broken it. A wet stickiness ran down, soaking his pants. He smelled it and felt the heat rising.

He managed to drag himself behind some large stacks of wood, where he felt safer. He wanted to howl from all the pain, scream out every cussword he knew in case it helped the pain pass, when he heard one, two, three shots. All of them up into the air, he could tell from the echo. Likely fired with the intent to scare him, so that he'd move and give away his position.

After the blast from the shots, he was enveloped by a silence and darkness unlike any he'd known. It wasn't long before he'd grasped everything around him, buzzing from certainty after certainty surging through his veins. It was clear now, he really was meant to be there. This was his life and his story, and though he felt weak and selfish, he realized he could no longer fight the inevitable. Before he passed out, he dreamed of the day he'd return there and throw his name up on both buildings, side by side. Loki.

# THE TRIP

FOR RAPHA, OF COURSE

I'd rolled into Arraial do Cabo hoping to ring in the New Year someplace calm. Far from the madness of Copacabana, where so many of my friends were planning to spend New Year's Eve. It was my first réveillon with Nanda. I was crazy about her. I hoped the trip would bring us even closer together, allowing us to experience things we couldn't as college students on Fundão Island. The place was beautiful, vibrant. A far cry from our recent past filled with assignment after assignment, endless photocopies, bills, anxiety, too little time.

We arrived and found Gabriel waiting for us. I felt happy knowing I'd spend the last few days of the year with him. Gabriel is my oldest friend, the person I'd shared all my very first secrets and discoveries with, and his company at a time of so much change was a relief. Some things really should stay the way they've always been. Right then, I needed that stability. Luckily, Nanda and Gabriel got along well with each other, which made it as easy for Gabriel to extend the invitation as it was for Nanda to accept it.

The house belonged to Gabriel's cousin Juan, an Argentinian. He was a happy, bumbling gringo, like too-blond gringos tend to be, at least when they're on vacation. When he was quiet, not jabbering on in Spanish, he had a certain charm. Except, what he liked most of all was to gab and laugh as loudly as possible. He really loved fine weed and had brought several baggies of top-notch asparagus with him, such that in under two hours we'd each smoked three blunts.

The house was modest and empty, a hidden nook in a beautiful setting, the perfect place to spend a few days just digging life. There were two bedrooms, a small bathroom, a kitchen that led to a living room, and a hammock hanging on the veranda. It was the first time I was in Arraial, and I couldn't wait to explore every centimeter of it.

Wanting to reciprocate their hospitality and fine bud, I pulled two squares of LSD out of my backpack. I asked Gabriel to grab me a pair of scissors so I could dole out the sugar cubes. When he saw what was happening, Juan jumped up all agitated, yelling in Spanish "No, no, no." He ran his hands over his head, spitting out words in sticky-tongued Spanish, and turned shrimp red. I was disturbed by what I saw. I looked over at Nanda, who also seemed confused. Was Juan one of those potheads who couldn't stomach other drugs, not even psychedelics?

Gabriel, on his way back with the scissors, burst into a deep, forceful chuckle when he realized what was going on. The weed we were smoking was far superior to what we were used to buying in the favelas that were easily accessed from Fundão; I say this to justify how mental I was, everything unfolding before me in slow motion.

Juan's voice echoed inside me, along with Gabriel's

laughter and Nanda's discomfort. Nervous and embarrassed, I felt like a real space cadet for wanting to drop acid at two in the afternoon, and for no other reason than our hangout.

What was Nanda thinking about everything going on? Did she see me as just another druggie wannabe artist, like so many others at our school? Gabriel's laughter seemed to go on forever, scattering to every corner of the kitchen and the living room, bouncing off windows and walls, buzzing back louder each time. When things finally quieted down, he told me that Juan was just begging me to please for the love of God save the sugar for New Year's Eve, that he didn't know where to get any around there and didn't want to miss the chance to trip balls as the fireworks went off. I was deeply relieved. I felt my breath returning to its usual rhythm. It's possible it all lasted no more than a minute, yet to me it had felt like hours. That bud really was a sucker punch to the brain.

I asked Gabriel to tell our host not to worry, that we'd be well and truly blasted as the ball dropped, high on good old bike 100. As Gabriel translated my message, I grabbed the two sheets of acid I had with me from my bag, primed to give us the mind melt we deserved, along with some cash to help out with any expenses. It felt good to not be a space cadet anymore, but a knight in shining armor.

The gringo got all excited. He looked adoringly at the colorful squares. It was a strange and beautiful sight. Gabriel let out another one of his thundering belly laughs, but this time it didn't frighten me or get me down; instead, I was infected by the powerful energy of his laughter, and joined in with my own chortle. Following suit, Nanda surrendered to the moment in a burst of high-pitched and syncopated laughter. After a long moment studying the tabs, Juan finally joined us. It was a happy and frantic sound. We were victims of a genuine Joker attack.

I cut the two squares into four (nearly) equal parts, and we each got (practically) half. We dropped the tab and could barely taste the bitterness in most acids. Nanda and I knew that, though flavorless, the stuff was fierce. We'd taken a quarter in my dorm room once and gotten mucho locos, babbling on about our childhoods, promising to be as honest to each other as we could, to not hide anything from one another, not even our most embarrassing or humiliating experiences. Then, I'd sketched her lying across the pillows resting against the windowed wall.

After about twenty minutes, our euphoria passed. We made a couple of passing remarks about psychedelic experiences, trying to explain one trip or another, but it's impossible to describe what happens after the acid drops, and soon we fell quiet, waiting for the next high to hit, enjoying the deep chill of the weed.

I already felt like blazing up again. Aside from the smooth taste of fresh bud, I was sure a blunt would help the psychedelic high ride in once and for all. I was too embarrassed to ask the gringo to skin up, and even more so to roll one myself with the crushed weed I was carrying in my pack.

I decided to light a cigarette. In that moment, I sensed it might inspire Juan to generate more smoke (we get all kinds of notions when we're stoned). Between one drag and the next I began to notice Juan was uneasy. He even stuffed his hands in his pockets, like he was looking for something. Since he couldn't find it, he started wandering around the living room, searching. I couldn't keep a small smile from creeping onto my face, thinking he was after some weed, indirectly influenced by the blue haze filling the living room, or telepathically compelled by the desire that had taken hold of me.

This illusion crumbled once I realized Juan had found what he was looking for, an enormous capsule filled with cocaine. Gabriel went bug-eyed and let out a burst of laughter.

As he set up the cola, the gringo offered us some and laughed. His eyes glimmered over the platter. It was almost depressing, and yet the task filled him with such happiness and satisfaction that he remained dignified as he carried out his function. Gabriel had never done coke. He takes it easy when it comes to drugs. Besides weed, he only drops acid and huffs lança-perfume (on special occasions). He asked for a bit to dust his tongue so he could feel his mouth go numb. Then he just stood there, curiously watching his cousin's passionate work.

Juan offered me a line, which I turned down: "No, no, muchas gracias." He immediately offered some to Nanda, his tone utterly gentle. I don't know how things work in Argentina, but, in these parts, we usually offer drugs (especially the hardest) only to those who we know use them regularly. I glanced at Nanda, trying not to communicate anything with my eyes, trying not to weigh in on her decision in any way. She looked briefly in my direction before accepting the line from the gringo.

My heart raced, I wasn't sure exactly why. I almost changed my mind and accepted a line of the white powder, but it was too late. I didn't want to seem like I was so easily influenced by Nanda. As I watched them sharing the straw they'd fashioned out of a two-real note, I felt jealous.

After that, we headed to the beach. Juan and Gabriel led the crew, talking animatedly in Spanish. I walked beside Nanda, locking into the rhythm of her steps. The high was starting to hit, and it rode in heavy. I was fascinated by the shape of my fingers, and admired them, thinking: "Whoa, we're just perfect, unique. Isn't it amazing to be alive, here, sending off another year of our life in this place full of trees and sky? The houses on this street are so beautiful! People's lives seem so chill here!"

Now and then Nanda sniffled. She wasn't used to doing coke. Honestly, I was kind of scared she'd get too blasted from mixing acid with powder, that she'd space and start getting paranoid about everything. Her expression was serious, impenetrable. I felt the need to know what was going on in her head.

"What do you think of Juan?" I asked.

"He's so wild. He doesn't understand a thing we're saying, and yet he goes on and on, laughing, playing. He's super intense. I think he really believes he's happy, and that's why he can experience his happiness so intensely."

"When you say 'so wild' do you mean 'so high'?" I continued.

"Everybody goes a bit overboard this time of year. Some with stress, others with love, anxiety, guilt, their quest for freedom. The truth is we become really vulnerable to ourselves. Juan's just surrendering to it, riding the waves of the weekend high. 'Cause this time of year always feels like the end of the world. And the end of the world either makes us want to live life till everything goes up in smoke and all we're left with is an empty silence, or it leaves us feeling disappointed. 'Cause we know that in the end we're just incomplete. That's why, when December comes along, we've got to stay strong."

"You think he's gay?"

"You're hilarious, Rafa. The gringo's really caught your eye all of a sudden, huh? Look, you might not know this about me yet, but I can get pretty jealous."

I was filled with an immense happiness when we reached the beach. I immediately dashed toward that crystalline water, which gathered in the distance into an infinite blue. Gabriel followed. Together, we dove into the smooth surf, laughing and swimming side by side. The water was chilly and the sun bright and hot, further proof that the universe was in total harmony.

Nanda sat on the beach, on her Ganesha sarong. Next thing I knew, she was already in her bikini. I was so mesmerized by the ocean that I didn't even think to keep tabs on Juan, to see if his gringo eyes lingered too long on Nanda's curves as she took off her clothes. I was expecting a glance at least, even from Gabriel. It's impossible not to watch the miraculous sight of a woman removing her clothing. I just wanted to check for any signs of a malicious glimmer in the gringo's eyes.

I looked out at both of them on the beach. Juan was tripping, watching the sky, nearly motionless, the sun hitting his face. Nanda's eyes were fixed on the ocean. Serious. She seemed to be contemplating the sheer existence of all that water and whatever incredible coincidence had allowed our atoms to come together in that place, in that exact moment. Sometimes Nanda thinks too much. Gabriel swam from side to side, diving, yelling. I've always found it beautiful to watch his body in the throes of freedom.

After a while, the gringo walked to the edge of the beach and looked out at the calm waves crashing before his eyes. Nanda was right, he always did everything with absolute devotion, whether laughing, smoking weed, snorting coke, watching waves. She was soaking up the sun, lying back, her body loose over the white sand. The gringo came running toward us in the water, laughing.

I became fascinated by all the many thousands of bluish hues that could fit into a single afternoon. I let my body float on the water, my eyes closed, felt the bright light and heat touching down on me, and thought: "Even though I've never been on this beach, I feel so close to this water, as if we'd met many, many times before on all the beaches I've ever visited, even rivers. We're amigos. That's why the water on this beach, which doesn't know me, really, is so fully accepting of my body and lets me be in harmony with all the other creatures of this aquatic universe."

When Nanda finally decided to join us in the water, it was a huge party. The four of us mucking about, laughing, competing to see who could dive the farthest to collect sand. Right then, we were all totally tripping and happy, buzzing from the joy of being able to spend that moment together. Even my jealousy and paranoia eased up.

It felt like we'd spent all summer long on that beach, so we said goodbye to that place, wanting to explore the rest of Arraial. It all happened really fast, I can't remember exactly when the decision was made. It was only as we neared the next beach that I started understanding what was going on. I was thrilled. That was exactly what I needed: to explore so I could transcend.

We walked for hours and hours that day and saw some

of the most beautiful beaches in the world. I was exhausted, my legs begging for rest. And yet I had within me a certain quasi-hallucinatory disposition that I was sure could carry me far beyond my usual limitations. I wondered how my travel companions were doing. I mean, what were they experiencing, deep inside them, in that very moment? It'd been a while since we'd communicated with words, instead using brief commands and bursts of laughter. Joker attacks that lasted an average of five minutes, sometimes longer, and gave us terrible and delicious bellyaches. We were blessed by a mysterious energy, I could practically touch it. Until Gabriel interrupted our moment of ecstasy by warning: "We should start heading back, it's getting dark."

We decided to walk back along the sand dunes. Juan assured us that, if we were fast, we could reach the town center before nightfall. I loved that idea. Walking over those white sand hills was amazing. How long had all those grains of sand been heaped up like that? What was the ancient form of each of those little granules, dispersed around the world, before they'd experienced their great transformation? How many rocks, crumbled by time, were needed to birth a dune?

It was in the middle of this thought that I realized we were being followed. I'd seen them before, two brawny blond dudes who looked like playboy gym rats, the "no pain, no gain" sort. They were a fair distance behind us. At first, I'd decided they were just on a walk in the area, but I soon noticed that the rhythm of their steps was synching with ours, that they were taking the same paths we were.

I didn't want to worry the others until I was sure there'd be trouble. Didn't want to be pegged as the paranoid crackpot who gets the crew all worked up. But the feeling of being followed kept growing inside me, suffocating me. Something really weird was about to go down, I felt this with the greatest certainty of all time. Positive we were gonna be jumped, I sounded the alert. Nanda and Gabriel were tickled when they saw the looks of the two miscreants: blond, well-fed. There was no avoiding it, I'd been pegged as the Crew Crackpot.

I dropped a *fuck this noise* and started running, pulling Nanda with me by the arm. She ran beside me yelling and laughing: "Are you bouldered, Rafa, baby, are you seeing stuff?" Juan and Gabriel stopped to watch the scene, but soon they were legging it too: the two dudes had stepped toward us. They were, in fact, members of the wellness generation and ran at a speed far superior to ours, on top of which they seemed familiar with the area, taking shortcuts that brought them closer and closer to us.

First, they reached Gabriel, who rolled in the sand with the mugger. Nanda ran beside me, terrified. In a (nearly) insignificant fraction of a second, we split. She took a path down, while mine led me up the sand dunes.

I had no clue where the gringo was, which would've been good to know, seeing as he was the strongest of us (physically), a key player in the scuffle that seemed to be taking shape.

The other guy was closing in on Nanda. This just couldn't be happening, not then, not like that. I swung toward the miscreant while instantly calculating the time and velocity needed for my body to slam against his.

It was an incredible sight, my shoulder colliding against the rival body. Thanks to the hatred I felt, my skinny and malnourished frame managed to level that lout. We fell and rolled in the sand. I felt like a quarterback knocking down his opponent in the most important game of his life. As fists started flying, Juan sprang up out of nowhere and ran off with Nanda.

I didn't know what to do in that fight, I was too confused to come up with any combat strategy, and just kept flailing and contorting to keep from being immobilized. When I finally managed to move away from my opponent and think even the slightest thought about the situation, I yelled:

"We've got nothing to lose, buddy, we were just digging the beach."

My rival responded by yelling to the other guy, who was grappling with Gabriel:

"Ay, ay, he's no gringo, man, this guy's no gringo!"

So Gabriel rose up, yelling:

"We're locals, man! You gotta respect locals. Shit!"

And so the gringo robbers split. Just like that. I know it seems like a lie, but that's life. Incredible. The worst of it all, though, was experiencing it with Nanda. What had happened would certainly reverberate throughout our relationship. But how?

We followed the path Nanda and Juan had taken. We weren't familiar with the area and felt totally disoriented, which made it impossible to plan any next steps. Then, we hit an enormous swamp. Night began falling over everything, and in a matter of minutes we couldn't see farther than a few centimeters. We walked carefully, calling out Nanda's and Juan's names. Nothing. Soon, I felt like crying. And then cried. Thankfully, the lack of light kept Gabriel from noticing. I couldn't make any coherent sense of the events, and just felt a heavy weight on my shoulders. It was the worst trip I could've ever imagined.

We reached the end of the swamp, the town center just

beyond it. The streets were deserted. No sign of Nanda or Juan. My heart beat frantically, hard and heavy at the thought of all the many tragedies that could've passed. Until Nanda called out my name from inside the pharmacy and I was finally able to breathe. Juan was with her. She'd gone into the shop to buy a vial of merthiolate, her legs covered in blood.

"We ran across the swamp before it got completely dark. I tripped through all the thorny bushes in the world. I could feel them slicing up my skin, making me bleed, but I wasn't in pain. At the time, I thought it was because my blood was hot, that I was frantic, scared as hell and, because of that, detached from my senses. It's so strange to be hurt, to be hurt and not feel any pain," Nanda said.

Juan was the same as when we'd met him earlier that day: happy and bumbling. He looked like he hadn't understood any of what had happened, and that he didn't want to understand. I just wanted to fall into bed and sleep. When I woke up, there'd only be two days left until that epic year's end.

# THE MYSTERY OF THE VILA

IN MEMORY OF DONA MARIA DE LOURDES

After the rain had come down—right on schedule—to cool the sweltering night, Ruan, Thaís, and Matheus scurried back onto the street, wanting to feel the wind that had been absent since early summer. Deep in the vila where they met lives Dona Iara, who, as one of the oldest women on the block, witnessed three generations of her family come of age on the land she helped tame. It is her house that the smell of macumba comes from.

The three friends manage to break up a game of footie forming between two speed humps, challenging the gaggle of kids to see who could get closest to Dona Iara's house, who could best catch the smell of macumba, hear loudest the ruckus of rats, bats, and bamboo creaking beyond the open sewer.

The children advance cautiously through the darkening vila. It barely resembles the vila it's always been, where during the day they shoot marbles, spin tops, and play tag. When it's macumba night, everything takes on an air of mystery: the babble of the bamboo grove, the running water, the shadows, the voices, the echoing of all things. The children shake with fear, and together savor every second of that early childhood terror.

Suddenly, one of the kids spooks and tears off. Then, the others run after; hearts race, smiles creep, they look at each other, conspirators, bursting with curiosity, wanting to discover the reason for the sudden dash.

"Y'all seen that, mané? A strange creature crawled outta the river. I saw this humongous shadow."

"I think it was the spirit's voice speaking."

Following the explanation, there's always at least one other kid who says that they saw or heard it, too, adding to the tension and pleasure of the adventure.

During the day, everybody greets Dona Iara, fetching her cigarettes or word on the bootleg lotto winner. Dona Iara is too old to be walking down to the corner, so she always sends a kid. Sometimes, she lets them keep the change or gives them a coin. On bright, sunny days, Dona Iara really does look like a saint: oh-so-black, oh-so-old, with honey-colored eyes. At night, she's transformed, by the smells, the wind, everything creaking with life.

"My dad says macumba's like weed: the devil's work! First syllable wouldn't rhyme with 'bad' if it was good."

"My mom says people who do macumba can do good things and bad things."

"My uncle got possessed by the spirit and ended up killing Magnus, his own dog! My aunt says they done macumba to him."

When Dona Iara built her shack on the riverbank, it was a nameless place with no aspirations of becoming a street.

With time, houses began popping up. Back then, her husband was still alive, his name was Jorge, and he was a pai-de-santo. He was the one who started holding meetings in the backyard of their house. Nearly all the neighbors took part in the gira, even Catholics who went to Sunday mass. But, with the passing of years, the number of attendants fell as the number of churches in the area grew. Dona Iara's terreiro was slowly forgotten and soon started being disparaged by its former regulars, once they'd converted. It was a hard blow for Dona Iara. After she was widowed, she even considered leaving that place, selling her house, starting afresh someplace new. But it was too late for that. Her roots were bound to that land. And so, she leaned on her memories for consolation.

Once, she had prayed for Matheus, who was burning up with fever. Back then, nearly his entire family had become believers, but the boy wasn't getting any better. The doctor couldn't fix him, the pastor's prayers couldn't fix him, so they called on the old woman. As she prayed and rubbed fresh herbs on the boy, his band of relatives sang out: "Hallelujah!" "Praise the Lord!" "He is the one true God!" When she finished her prayer, Dona Iara took a sip of cachaça and told everyone to do the same. They did, and then she said the boy would be well. Matheus's parents said yes, that God was with them, that it was only a scare. Once the old woman left, Matheus's relatives, peppered throughout the corners of the room, spent a long while looking at each other, and made a silent pact to never speak on the streets of what had happened that night. Matheus spoke of it only to Ruan, who spoke of it to no one.

Another time, Ruan's house was infested with ticks. All

sorts of ticks, all over the place. They crawled up walls, the sofa, they even crept over the saints. Everyone was just waiting on the time when the dog would die, every last drop of its blood drained. Dona Iara went there, killed three of the parasites, placed them inside a matchbox, and told Ruan's grandmother to cast it at a crossroads. The grandma left, taking the boy with her. Ruan spoke of it only to Matheus, who spoke of it to no one.

Thaís's entire family are Jehovah's Witnesses, except for her dad, who's a drunk. She isn't allowed to go to the corner to buy cigarettes, or to play bootleg lotto for Dona Iara, which is why she never gets to keep the change or get any coins. She can't donate blood or eat sweets on the day of Saints Cosmas and Damian, she can't even have a birthday party. What no one imagines is that, when she was inside her mama, struggling to enter the world on account of a knotty birth, it was Dona Iara who worked to unknot her mama's belly. Thaís's mother never breathed a word of it to a soul.

After the fright, the running, the smiles, the glances, the children are all drawn back to the danger. Creeping, gripping at the pebble-dash wall, hiding behind the mango tree and the empty water tank. With each step, their hearts beat harder, their breaths trip over each other. It's a party. They know that in the end it'll be a good story, the subject of spirited conversations shared outside Galo Cego bar.

One night, a loud noise cut through the din. It was the door. The children smiled desperately, waiting. Mílton, one of Dona Iara's sons, ran through the vila, sweating, nervous, and didn't even spy the children, hidden away, as he ran to the street. "He's possessed," they said. Through the open door, the smell of macumba gusted out stronger than ever. The children trembled, not daring to leave their hiding place.

Matheus's uncle's car stopped at the vila gate, Mílton ran back home, and the parked car sat waiting. The children looked on without understanding. Tucking themselves between curiosity and fear, they watched the scene unfold. Then the two sons walked out carrying their unconscious mother in their arms. Ruan and Thaís felt an intense urge to cry, and so hugged. The car flew off, carrying Dona Iara to the hospital.

None of the kids knew what to think or do. They stared down at the ground, their words labored.

"I think I saw Mílton crying."

"Are we gonna leave the door open?"

One thing was true: that time, there'd be no lively conversations outside Galo Cego. The night had been cut short, suspended by a different fear, absent of pleasure. Ruan went over to shut the door; then, in silence, they all set off home.

On the following day, since Dona Iara's sons had stayed in the hospital, it was Matheus who broke the news, relaying everything he'd heard from his uncle. It was a heart attack. Or a stroke, who knows. One of those things old people die from. "She's been hospitalized. She nearly died." This was what he knew.

Thaís spent all week praying to Jehovah for Dona Iara's life and spoke of it to no one. She included the old woman in all her daily prayers; she even prayed for her at congregation and at their Sunday meeting, even though she didn't know whether it might be a sin to pray for a macumbeira in the Lord's house.

Ruan was glum, holed away at home, playing on his own, without a sound or a smile. His grandma, seeing the boy's sadness, asked if he'd had a tiff with his friends.

"I don't want Dona Iara to die, Grandma. Remember when she came over and chased away all those ticks? If she hadn't helped, Máilon would be dead today, his blood all gone. I remember."

Touched, his grandma suggested:

"Well, then pray to God for her, my boy. Or better yet, pray to a saint. If you have faith, he'll help you with God. When saints ask, the Lord always answers."

The boy stood facing the altar at home, staring carefully at those icons, trying to believe they really could help. Ever since he was a young boy, he'd lived with those figurines, never asking them for a thing. Our Lady of Aparecida, Saint Francis of Assisi, and Saint George were all there. Ruan thought first of asking Aparecida, because she looked so like Dona Iara, but he soon gave up on that idea. He looked at her figure and the words just didn't come out. He looked at Saint George, this time seeing his armor, the way he conquered that dragon, and was certain that if Saint George could slay a real-live dragon with just a horse and a sword, he could do anything in the world. Without realizing, words started pouring freely from him to the saint. He made his request and his promise, offered thanks in advance, and said his goodbyes.

Even after they returned to the street and to their games, Ruan and Thaís never once stopped praying. Matheus was the one who seemed not to care. When he shared news from the hospital, it was with pleasure, happy to be the object of so much attention. Until Ruan couldn't handle his friend's indifference any longer and spat out, in front of everyone:

"You don't give a damn about Dona Iara, even after she prayed for you when you were sick with fever!"

Matheus looked at Ruan with spite, he couldn't believe he'd exposed his family's secret. Ruan clenched his fists. If Matheus denied it, he'd have at him. But Matheus didn't say a word. He turned his back, leaving the game behind.

It was almost telenovela time when Dona Iara arrived by taxi with her two sons. The car stopped at the gate. She stepped out, propping herself up on both men, and they walked, their steps slow, into the vila. The children scattered home, eager to share the good news. They'd all seen her walk out of the cab.

The following morning, Ruan and Thaís went to Matheus's house to apologize and invite him to visit Dona Iara with them. Matheus accepted their apologies, but said he'd rather stay home playing video games. Ruan said that, if that was the case, he could forget about the apology, that he needn't bother ever looking him in the eyes again. Then, since they were best friends after all, Matheus paused his game and followed his friends into the vila.

When the children arrived, Dona Iara was lying in bed, dressed head-to-toe in white; she really did look like a saint. Ruan immediately spotted a flaming candle right above their heads, beside a glass of water, just like his grandma did every week. The whole house had an odd smell to it, pleasant but stuffy. The light was scarce, yet there was just enough to shine on Dona Iara, who glowed in bed, despite her tired eyes.

"Dona Iara, I prayed so much to Jehovah for you," Thaís said, feeling she had to say something, then kissed the old woman's head. She was very nervous about being there, inside that house.

"Thank you, my daughter. It's thanks to God that I'm alive today."

It was very strange to hear the macumbeira speak of God. Dona Iara saw the children's wonder and spoke again. She spoke of how things had gone in the hospital, where she'd been more frightened of death than she'd ever imagined. Then she recounted stories from when she'd first arrived on the street where they live, the look of the trees and of the river before it became a sewer, its waters running clean and proper for bathing and fishing. The festival of Kings, Carnaval, São João. The children listened attentively to these words, picturing everything. Then she told the story of certain orishas, and it was all so exciting and action-packed that they felt as if they were all three watching a movie on TV. Next thing they knew, they had to go, the morning had flown past and it was time for lunch. Before they left, Ruan spoke of the promise he'd made to Saint George. Dona Iara laughed, content:

"My boy, I always did tell your grandma you were Ogum's son!"

They hugged and kissed Dona Iara and left easily, as if they'd been in and out of that house many times before. On their way back, as they crossed the street, not one of the three children spoke of it.

After Dona Iara got better, they went back to playing on days that smelled of macumba. Everything was very much as it had been before, except for Ruan, who, as he played, feared having to lie. From then on, when the children scattered onto the street, Ruan would infiltrate the vila on his own, clinging to the walls and hiding in shadows until he reached the door, knocked, and entered to hear the many stories of the Sacred Warrior, his Protector, Ogum iê, his Father.

# PADRE MIGUEL STATION

Back then, crack was outlawed in Vintém. Things had gotten out of control: tons of theft, brawling, disturbances. Crack's fucked up. What it fetches in money, it fetches in trouble for the folks working the bocas. It's even worse for locals, because for them it's just perrengue, shame, worry. One thing's for certain: no way would the traffickers stop selling, they'd gotten too used to the profits they got from the rock. The solution they hit on was to lay down a law banning crack use in the neighborhood. I can't honestly remember if it covered the entire favela or if it was just around the train tracks, where shit was more chaotic.

On the train tracks, I'm sure it was off-limits. So much so there wasn't a soul in sight when we got there. Only thing left of Cracolândia was the trash and the stench: Guaravita cups, rags, cigarette filters, human shit, empty lighters. We sat on the tracks, which are always cleaner than the walls that run the length of the train line to the station. Night had just fallen, which back when crack was legit used to be rush hour. People coming from work, from school, folks stepping off the train or camped out in the favela all gathered together. The night offered protection to anyone who didn't want to explain their addiction. To those walking past outside in the dark, everybody on the train tracks was nameless, faceless—just a bunch of addicts.

I didn't smoke there anymore. Besides the smell of filth, after a while that meeting of people hungering for rocks started making me feel queasy. I'd only go there when I had to take the train somewhere; I'd toke up quick, then walk straight up to the station. It's funny, 'cause in the heyday of crack on the streets of Bangu, I made and laughed at crackhead jokes just like anybody else. But the truth is whenever I spent too long in Cracolândia, I'd start picturing their lives before the rock and feel like crying.

I'll never forget this woman I met on the train. First, she tried selling me an umbrella, then she started telling me about how her whole family was from Alagoas, and that she'd left them all behind to come to Rio with her husband, to try to make a life for themselves, because it was tough for him to get a job up there. She also told me how, right after they got here, she gave birth to a daughter and that she's nine years old today. She said sometimes he comes down to these tracks, takes her home, washes her, beats her, locks every door. But it's no use, she always manages to run away from her family. Then she started crying. She bawled, her mouth open, snot running down her nose, not in the least embarrassed by my being there, watching her. As the woman sobbed, I scrutinized what teeth she had left, wondering if her story was true or if she was just trying extra hard to move me so I'd give her some money. "He's a good man, he deserves a better woman than me," she said, and then asked for a hug. The tears running down her cheeks looked real, and since I didn't have any money in my back pocket, I gave in.

◆

"This two-real bud's always wack when it comes in this black baggie," I said, as I started working on the weed.

"For real, the good stuff comes in yellow packs. Remember the time when you could roll two sweet blunts with a single baggie's worth?" Rodrigo was always talking about that time, and I was always agreeing, even though I wasn't sure I could in fact remember; the color of two-real baggies was always changing in Vila Vintém. Besides Rodrigo and me, there was also Felipe, Alan, and Thiago. Back then, we were attached by the hip and always went together, no matter the mission. I didn't have a clue what I wanted to do with my life, but knew whatever it was, it'd be with them.

The plan was to swing by Vintém, blaze, then take the train to Bangu to visit Léo's new baby girl. Another one of our crew who'd gone and become a dad. I remember how, mission-bound, that night was the first time I wondered whether the friendships we forged in our teenage years could survive adult life.

"This grass is a joke, for real. Check it, feel that ammonia burning your throat?" Alan said soon after rolling the blunt.

"Fucks you up sometimes, though. I've smoked this sort of bud loads, and at the end of the joint everybody's always limp-faced. What matters is for it to get you fired up," Thiago replied, chill as could be, slicking some spittle onto the joint so it burned slower.

It didn't work. Even spittled and breezeless, the joint burned fast on account of the dry weed, didn't even make it around the ring twice. And all of us still straight.

"We gotta roll another. We walked all the way here, I wanna get high," Rodrigo said, prepping a napskin.

Felipe was the crew's missionary. He took the train and went anywhere he needed to get good bud. In the time we've known each other, he's been locked up near five times, and gone through some dark stuff. Even so, the numbers were in his favor; if he were to count all the times he'd chased weed far from his hood and got away with it, five times was nothing. He recited his usual spiel:

"That's why I'm always saying we gotta get some cash together and buy our shit in Jaca, Mangueira, Juramento, Antares, I dunno, mano, good grass. That's what I want. Smoking this stepped-on junk is rough."

"You're right, meu mano, I agree with you. But it's gotta be for a sweet package. If we're just buying ten reals' worth of bud we should do it here, close to home," Thiago said.

I'd heard that conversation a million times and was positive the next thing Felipe would say was:

"That's what I'm saying, man. We each put down ten and buy ourselves a pack of fifty so we can lay back and chill."

I smiled at how spot-on my prediction was. Sometimes those regurgitated conversations really got under my skin, 'cause they made it seem like things were always the same, day in, day out. But sometimes I'd get involved and, in those moments, I took pleasure in those fixed dialogues.

"You guys only ever talk about drugs, never seen a thing like it."

"That's 'cause the world's doped up, brother. It's almost

like you hadn't heard. I've told you once, I'll tell you again: one week without drugs and Rio de Janeiro grinds to a halt. No doctors, no bus drivers, no lawyers, no cops, no street sweepers, nothing. Everybody bugging out, cold turkey. Cocaine, Rivotril, LSD, pills, crack, weed, Novalgin, whatever, mano. Drugs are what this city runs on."

Alan loved to talk about that stuff, and we loved listening to him.

"Drugs and fear," I concluded.

Mid-banter, we were already on our third blunt, and nothing. Just a weird pressure in my head, dizziness. I kept wondering if Léo's wife, Amanda, wouldn't be pissed if a bunch of stoners rolled up to her house reeking of ammonia. Must be eight p.m., at least. I wanted to alert the crew, but decided to let it be. They'd just say Amanda was real chill, that she'd always gotten on with the gang. And it was true. The girl was as mental as we were. Before her daughter was born, we used to hang out all the time with her and Léo in Lapa, and she was always one of the wildest when we ran out of Coca-Cola and the time came to drink straight vodka. In any case, kids change people, and I wondered whether they'd want us to stop by some other time, some other day.

"Lua vai iluminar os pensamentos dela, fala pra ela que sem ela eu não vivo, viver sem ela é o meu pior castigo . . ."

"Vai dizer . . ."

The song rang out from the bar behind the station. I can't quite remember when or how, I think Felipe started leading the crew along to Katinguelê's lyrics and we followed him, clapping, spreading our arms, cracking up. Until we fell into absolute silence.

I never understood that stuff. I mean, I've always felt

deeply uncomfortable with inexplicable silences. It's always as if something were breaking. From one moment to the next, everything comes undone, collapses, and we're left on our own, faced with the abyss of another person. Then, you feel like saying something or other just to try and sweep up all these pieces of people, half a dozen fragments scattered by our mysterious coexistence.

"I'll go to Jacaré tomorrow, then. Y'all's mission is to get hold of ten reals each, before noon, that's when I'll be heading. Don't worry about the ticket, it'll be courtesy of SuperVia," Felipe said.

"Go earlier, fool. The sun's fierce at noon. If you make it back fast we can even hang at the waterfall in Barata," I said.

"You out of your mind, dude? The a.m. trains are lose-lose. Commuting time's grim, from here to Central they just pack you in tighter and tighter."

"Go later in the a.m., mano. Shit's chill by nine, you can even get a seat. Noon's when it's rough. And you risk getting stuck with a full train on the way back."

All that back-and-forth was just an attempt to get us to where we'd been. To normal.

"All right, then. I'll leave at nine. Y'all got cash on you?"

"Nah, man, still got to parley that out at home."

"I've got money in my account. Dad's pension came in today. When we get to Bangu, I'll take some out at the ATM. Then, this is what you'll do: go buy the weed, take your part, and leave the rest with me. Then, when y'all give me the dough, I'll hand over what's yours, got it? But, check it, if y'all don't put money down, like last time, don't even bother begging, I ain't saving you. I've told you before, if you don't pay up, only Jesus saves."

All that talk was getting me down, I knew what we'd end up deciding and I knew they did, too. Which is when, out of the blue:

"Hell, don't know if I've told y'all this before, but there was this time when I went to Jaca, this was a while ago now, I'd cleaned up good, so the cops wouldn't suspect nothing. Plenty of plainclothes rolling by the trains back then, I remember. So I went there, right, I was even wearing shades. Except, when I get near the tracks, a crackhead rocks up outta nowhere, I swear, no clue where she came from, if she just walked straight through the station wall, or if she popped out of a manhole, all I know is I was spooked. Then she started staring at me, looking me up and down with these, like, fiendish eyes, I swear, don't laugh, man, I'm serious, that junkie wanted to seduce me! Then she came out with: 'Blow you for a fiver.' And I said I was good, thanks. Then you know what she said? Said she'd blow me for free."

"And you let her?"

"Nah, man, I got outta there."

"Check you out, breaking doped-up hearts all over Jacaré!"

"Bet you she would of asked for the dough after sucking you off, though. For sure. Then, if you didn't give it to her, she'd of gotten you into some mad trouble."

"You think I don't know that?"

"Y'all really think a fiver's too steep for the best buff of your life? Contemplate this: crackhead takes one look at your junk, sees a piece of five-real candy, and clocking that goes down on you hard, with gusto. And there's something else, too, none of those Jaca junkies got teeth, her little velvet mouth would of swallowed you savage, no pain."

We only stopped laughing because the train was coming our way and we had to get up. I kept wondering if we weren't already high and if this high wasn't the kind of high where you don't think you're high, like on my birthday when Vítor dropped a tab for the first time and kept yelling, all night long, so everybody at the party could hear: "I DON'T FEEL ANYTHING!"

It's always easier to tell if the high has hit when you stand up. Often enough you'll smoke for a long time and not feel a thing and then when you get up, you realize you're totally baked. After the train cleared us, everybody sat back down, except for me. I kept feeling things out. I couldn't understand what was going on, and that was starting to bother me.

I had this weird feeling when I sat back on the tracks, a kind of agony. An urge to get up and walk off, to follow my own path. Alone. Suddenly, the air had vanished, I couldn't remember how to breathe. I looked at my body, sweat trickling down. I quickly realized I was kicking off a bad trip or, who knows, a green-out, but I was too embarrassed to tell the gang and so I just stood there, unmoving, just focusing on getting my breath back.

I couldn't believe it, me, who was always so proud of having never smoked bad bud. My motto was: "You can't fight the high. If it comes on strong, just let it take you. Ride the tide, surf the wave." I've seen people who think they're going to suffocate after smoking more than they can take, calling home in the middle of the night, minds fried on acid, running after people, huffing loló. I always laughed at those sorts of trips, and my friends would say: "Your time will come! Everybody's does."

Little by little, my blood pressure went back to normal. I looked over at the guys and felt like I was seeing them for the first time that night. I was back. It was like I'd quit that scene and left behind only my body, empty. It was completely bizarre. And yet, what had felt really intense and frightening to me seemed not to have existed for any of my friends, right there next to me. They hadn't noticed a thing. Was all that connection I thought I felt thrumming between people just in my head? Was the hard truth of the matter that we're born and die alone, and never share our inner life with another being?

There was a time when I couldn't smoke on the street 'cause I always felt like I was being watched, that everybody was judging me. To be fair, it'd always been like that. With everything. Whenever something embarrassing happened— when somebody cussed me out for something I had or hadn't pulled, when my dick got hard on the bus for no reason—I always had the feeling people were watching me. But pot paranoia's the worst, it felt impossible to escape anyone's eyes, everybody seemed to be zeroing in on everything I did. Little by little, I broke free of that. These days, I know that on the street no one can really see us. Our pain, our addictions, our vexations—it's all too distant.

It reached me, the last joint, before we set off. I took it, acting natural. I'd overcome my unease, and no one had to be any wiser. I smoked half-heartedly, it tasted disgusting. Sometimes I wondered if it was worth smoking weed that was bad, old, dry, laced with ammonia. And I always kept at it, 'cause life seemed to be telling me that smoking was better than not. Even despite all the perrengue with the cops, my family, that kind of thing. When my friends and I met up to burn a blunt, there was this feeling that life could be good, that it didn't have to be that crazy shit they teach us as kids, all the rushing about, the stuffiness.

As we got up to leave, I felt tired. I didn't want to visit anybody or go to the square. I just wanted to go home, sleep, wait for tomorrow to arrive, and not think about a thing.

But suddenly one of Rodrigo's friends rocked up, this guy who's from the 77th. He greeted the crew. He'd asked for a sheet of notebook paper, but it took me a while to realize, because of his thick stammer. It was only when Rodrigo pulled a notebook out of the bottom of his backpack that I realized he was planning to smoke a zirrê with the two fools waiting behind him.

"If y-y-y'all wanna smoke a s-s-skinny before y-y-y'all s-s-split, just h-h-hit me up, k? This rock's p-p-p-p-puny."

I wanted to ask if he knew you couldn't smoke crack on the tracks anymore, but in the end I let it be. Everybody knew; if they wanted to get themselves into that mess, that was on them, who was I to be keeping tabs?

"Thanks, mano. That's solid, but we're gonna head. This grass's chaff, we've smoked shitloads and still feel straight. This junk's only good to smoke with gravel."

That's what I said, wanting to get out of there ASAP. Glancing to my side, I spotted a woman over the way smoking out of a Guaravita cup. I thought: "That's it, the favela's never gonna be the same after crack. No way to keep a handle on so many addicts."

"Pô, we should get in on that. Last round. Add that to this butt-end here and roll ourselves a mad-sweet spliff."

I didn't even bother answering. I knew that, no matter

what I said, we'd end up smoking that blunt. I also didn't want to come off as being too bouldered, or scared, because what I felt wasn't fear, it was just the need to leave. "Okay," I thought. "Dry as this weed is, won't take us ten minutes to shred, roll, toke, and split."

I was already at the other end when two dudes rolled up on a motorbike, the passenger with an AK-47 strapped across his chest and the driver a pistol at his waist. After that, everything happened double-quick, next thing I knew we were all standing against the wall, the AK pointed at our faces, the thug yelling:

"Y'all fucking crazy? Y'all retards? You wanna fucking die? Don't you know you can't smoke crack anymore in this shit?"

I was about to say we were just smoking weed when the junkie shrieked back at him:

"For God's sake, mister, I'm pregnant!"

I responded to this information by glancing at the small bump poking out from her skeletal frame. It was true.

"Shut the fuck up, you crazy ho, shut up! If you want your kid to live, don't be smoking this crap."

Driver didn't even get off, he just held the bike upright and watched things go down. Except, he pulled out his gun and cocked it to show everybody he was in it, too. As if he had to, as if we stood a chance against that AK if it set to serenading us.

"I just wanna know one thing: who wants to go first?"

And he pointed the AK's muzzle at our faces, lingering for a moment or so on each of us. When he got to the end, Thiago said:

"Shit's fucked now."

I'd never seen so much fear plastered across my friends' faces. And we've been through plenty of perrengues together. All I wanted to know was what would happen if, in that moment, we stopped existing, how our world would react, the people who worried about us. I remembered then how my mom had said to always keep my ID on me, 'cause if something happens and you don't, you go down as a John Doe. As usual, I didn't have mine.

At the bar, the pagode tunes kept on playing, indifferent to our situation. As I listened to the patrons' voices mingling with the music, I understood everything: it was terror. They were terrorizing us. If they'd meant to kill us, they would've taken us someplace else, somewhere specific. They wouldn't just leave our bodies there, strewn over the train tracks. They also weren't planning to drag us into the favela and set us on fire or dump our bodies some other way. On top of that, on the other side of the thin wall we were lined up against, plenty of locals hung about soaking up their pagode tunes and drinking beer. If they shot at us, the bullets would no doubt pierce through those walls and strike a local. And if I knew that, no way the lunatic with the AK didn't. It was all about terror.

I paid zero attention to anything else the thug yelled at us. I'd taken control of the situation, now all I had to concern myself with was keeping that look of terror in my eyes, as a sign of respect. This was no time to seem confident, no way could I let myself break into that smirk I get every time I realize that all the tension around me will come to nothing.

It wasn't long before he belted at us to scram, hailing bullets into the sky, as if he were signaling the beginning of a strange and desperate race. In a split second, we were all dashing as fast as we could toward the train, even the pregnant woman, who ran heavy, gripping her belly. I don't know how those scrawny legs didn't break on impact with the concrete. I watched my friends moving farther and farther from me, as I lost speed, thinking: "Someday I'll write this story."

# THE BLIND MAN

Seu Matias was born blind. He's never seen the ocean or guns or women in bikinis. Even so, he keeps on living life, and cruises all over as if the world were made for people like him. People who can't see, but who listen, smell, touch, feel, and speak.

And, in his case, speak powerfully. Seu Matias's job is to touch bus passengers' hearts. To achieve this goal, he plays a game of words and harrowing sounds with them, his voice mixing with the clamor of the city, the clinking of the coins rattling in his Guaravita cup, his tin cane always swinging left then right over the bus floor.

Everything hinges on how each potential patron's day is going. On whether it's the beginning or end of the month, whether they've eaten well or poorly, believe in God or not, are vulnerable to feeling, or guarded against the outside world. And yet, even considering all these factors, Seu Matias manages to pocket a decent amount of money every week, always working one day on, one day off.

As a kid, Matias couldn't stand the company of other

children. They were always prattling on at a ridiculous pace, trampling through topics, their voices jumbled, images spilling over each other; their words always flew far, far away. For this reason, he preferred talking to old men, who always had the patience to meticulously explain the shape of each thing, and with the degree of care only lonely old men can muster. The sky, rivers, rats, the rain, kites flying high, the rainbow, all those things we say throughout the day without a second thought to how they appear.

He soon memorized the hill's pathways, and began playing alone on those narrow streets, like a person whose eyes are parted only slightly, pretending to be blind, listening to the sounds of life bustling around him, picking up the smell of women's perfume, young men's weed, of lunch and sewage, happy to uncover his very own stories, without feeling he had to share them with anyone.

When he was six, his father went missing, vanished. The dominant theory was that he'd been killed for becoming a good-for-nothing. Which isn't hard to believe considering the state he got himself in when he boozed too hard. Several times, he'd ended up in the boca, and by the look of things, there'd been a ditch with his name on it for a while. What's weird about the whole thing is that no one on the hill breathed a word about it, no one knew a thing. It was all left unresolved, a mystery hanging in the air; they never did find the man's body.

Even years later, there was always somebody popping up claiming they'd seen Raimundo god-knows-where, doing god-knows-what. The truth is he wasn't missed at home. Dona Sueli, who was always swearing that if the beatings didn't stop she'd slip scalding water into that bastard's ear, could rest easy, certain she wouldn't have to fulfill her promise. What they did miss was the money he used to bring home, because, truth be told, when he wasn't drinking or getting himself into trouble, the son of a bitch was working. And even though the cash that made it past the bar all the way to the kitchen table wasn't much, it was enough that Dona Sueli had to double her workday, leaving in the morning and coming home at night, and putting up with her neighbors' malicious remarks.

Matias's siblings drifted apart slowly and naturally. Marcos got himself an older woman, with a kid and everything, and moved in with her. The youngest, Mariana, got herself a belly and moved in with the baby's daddy. When illness brought Dona Sueli down, only Matias stood by her side. Her neighbors, the same ones who used to tell tales, started caring for Dona Sueli. A few times a day, as they helped the old lady go to the bathroom, or fed her as she lay in bed, they asked what her other kids were up to that they couldn't look after their mother at a time like this. Dona Sueli always responded, implacable: "I didn't raise my kids for myself. I raised them for the world!"

After his mother's burial, walking back from the cemetery with his neighbors, Matias thought of what he'd do to get ahead. He'd have to keep feeding himself day after day and couldn't think of a single job that suited him. He refused to stand on the street rattling a can of coins, as had been suggested. He thought that if he was going to be asking, it should be by communicating with people, by telling his story.

He spent days rehearsing what he'd say when he stood before his audience of bus passengers. He spoke of his mother, of his missing father. Of how difficult it was for a blind man to get a job in the city. And, finally, he asked God to bless everyone there, both those who could and couldn't contribute.

He soon left home to ride buses and started living off the change he received from those moved or troubled by his speech. It all seemed easy in the beginning, the money rolled in, he knew his story by heart, split perfectly into separate sections. But little by little the truth revealed itself. The experience of reciting his own story day after day grew more and more painful, and living off charity became a kind of torment.

His loneliness weighed on him. Matias became quite close to a boy everybody called Doodle and who they all assumed would grow up to be a thug. The kid was constantly racing about, working as a runner, bringing meals to the dealers, buying cola for the junkies. Then, he spent his dough rolling blunts at the same boca he'd bought the weed from, to make himself known. One day, Matias invited him to come along with him on the bus. Soon enough, Doodle's presence was doubling donations. At a quick glance, the boy even looked like Matias—and everybody so pities a blind man's son. Doodle soon realized he made much more money with Matias on the bus than as a runner on the hill, and that it made his mom much happier.

As years passed, the kid's presence began to have less effect, some passengers even went so far as to say that a boy that size should be laying down slabs, putting up walls. Seu Matias decided to continue on his own, his increasingly apparent old age having become handy in his line of work. At sixteen, Doodle managed to rent a bike and started driving a mototaxi. During the time they had worked together, the two of them never had much to say to one another; even so, after they ended their partnership, Doodle didn't pull away completely from Seu Matias. At the end of his workday, the boy heads to the boca and buys all the weed and cocaine he can with the old man's money, then they sit around, smoking and snorting the night away in an agonized banter throughout which their eyes never meet.

# TGIF

When my old lady found out I was smoking, she didn't chew me out like I thought she would. Instead, she just said she wouldn't be giving me any money anymore, that if I was old enough to have an addiction, I was old enough to work to support it, too. I was reeling in the moment, but then I understood she was legit. It's like people say: "If your kid's ass is hairy, that makes you an ape."

The first job I got was as a ball boy for Márcio, a tennis instructor who lived upstairs. He taught at a few condominiums in Barra da Tijuca, and we'd have to leave the house at five thirty a.m. at the latest because after that, between six and ten, Avenida Niemeyer only ran in the opposite direction. Márcio was real fly and we swapped some fine notions on the ride over there. Even though we were on our way to work with tennis, soccer was always our subject of choice.

With the money I made, I could buy some stuff for myself and also help my ma out with the groceries. On the first night after I bought myself a pair of Nikes, I even wore them to bed. I'd walk down the street staring at my feet, watching the soles touch the ground, buzzing with joy. Better yet was when I stepped into school, I felt cool as shit, seemed like everyone had frozen in place just to watch me walk in. Another thing I remember from back then was the sense that I was helping out around the house for the first time, and how that changed the way my family treated me. It all felt so good, I wanted to keep on working forever, that's what I thought when I got home; but, when I arrived at the condominiums and grabbed that tube I used to collect tennis balls, stepped onto the court and felt the sun roasting my head, forced to serve people who didn't even look me in the eyes—in those moments, I never wanted to have to count on anyone in my life.

I started hating every single one of them. The old folk and the young ones, too, those I hated the most. I'd run after those balls, picturing how I'd respond to the crap they were spewing and that I was forced to listen to. Everything about them rubbed me the wrong way, the way they walked, talked, laughed, how they treated the employees, but what I hated the most was when they moaned about their problems: my maid didn't show up today, I had to take my car to the mechanic, I can't stand taking English classes anymore, our neighbor's dog was yapping all night long.

Sometimes, I'd still be throbbing with rage when I got to school, but then I'd meet up with my friends, we'd chew the fat, and the feeling would begin to pass. At home, all I remembered was the good stuff: money in my pocket, food on my plate, not having to do the dishes. Until one day on the court, everything exploded. A tennis student more or less my age came up to share a little quip with me, said I looked like some dude in a cartoon. I said to him: "Fuck you, bro. I ain't one of your lil condo pals!" The kid looked at me all scared, like he couldn't believe my spunk. Just then, I couldn't either.

Márcio was really pissed, said I nearly fucked up his job situation. My mom was pissed, everyone was furious. But, for me, the worst thing of all was that Márcio stopped talking to me. He was the one who took me to a soccer stadium for the first time, I'll never forget. For a while afterward, every time Flamengo kicked one straight into the net, I'd think about him and feel like knocking on his door, yelling together, giving him that hug pals do when their team scores.

I had several jobs after that one, but it was rough. Not only do you have to shave, cut your hair, be on time all the time, spend most of the day doing stuff for other people, you also got to keep a cool head. I couldn't hold anything down, and stuff at home got real weird sometimes. Living with my stepdad wasn't easy; sometimes we'd talk loose, others it seemed like there was only room for one of us in that house. My ma always took my side, in her own way, but she did. I know it drove her crazy how intolerant I could be, she was always saying: "Those who can, give orders, and those who are wise obey them." Like hell, I thought.

I came to passing out flyers through a buddy of mine from school. It was supposed to be a quick gig, just to tide me over for a while, but I've been at it for nearly a year now. The pay is skimpy, thirty reals a day, Monday to Friday, eight o'clock to four. To compensate, the work's easy: all I have to do is hand out leaflets to anyone who walks by, if folks take them, great, I don't care whether they dump them on the ground or go off searching for the offices to ask for a loan. If they don't take them, life goes on, one thing we've plenty of is people to keep trying with. A good thing about this gig is that I don't have to talk to anybody, I've got time to think and to plan and to picture the future.

The first day was weird. I'd overslept and gotten to the meeting place with seconds to spare. There were already some people waiting around, a bunch of homeless folk, a girl in the family way, an elderly woman who looked older than my grandma. I wasn't sure that was where I was meant to be waiting, my friend hadn't arrived yet. I lit a cigarette and tried to make sense of what I was getting myself into. My buddy arrived, confirming that was where we were meant to meet, we waited another ten minutes, and then the boss showed up. He asked for my name, handed me a stack of leaflets, and told me to pass them out on the corner of Rua da Carioca, just before you reach Tiradentes Square. So, there I went.

At first, I was real embarrassed. People walked past like they felt sorry for me, or were angry, hell knows. Sometimes, when I spotted someone approaching me, I'd make eye contact and gear myself up to hand them the flyer; in a way, in those moments, I felt like those people would've preferred I didn't exist. Trouble was, I took it personally, the way they looked at me. It was a while before I realized that those looks, whatever they meant, weren't directed at me, but at the leaflet distributor. Which is not who I am, no one is.

It was smooth sailing once I grasped that difference. Except for when someone I knew walked past. When that happened, I felt like sinking into the pavement. The first time was with a kid I knew from the hill. I spotted him in the distance walking down the sidewalk. I thought of getting out of there, but it was around the time the boss came by. I decided to stay where I was, my head hung low, so he wouldn't see me. Then I lifted my head, thinking he'd already walked past, and there he was, waiting to talk to me. I tried to hide the leaflets, but there was no use. I said to him: "I've been hustling, cuz." He told me things were tough for him, he was looking to hustle, too, that he might hit me up, see if I could hook him up with this gig. Then we hugged and he told me to come by his place sometime to play video games. Another time, it was real rough, my heart started racing like crazy, like it was gonna shoot outta my mouth. It was this girl from Cruzada São Sebastião who I'd been chatting up online for ages. It'd been a real struggle getting her to trust me, if she saw me now, I'd be done for. I knew it wouldn't work to stay put, so I just kept on passing out flyers, business as usual, and everything was fine, she just walked past, dead easy.

With my first week's pay, I decided to go to Jacarezinho to get myself some bud. It'd been a while since I had any weed on me, I only ever smoked when a buddy threw some my way. This time I wanted to put down for a fat package so I could give back to everybody who'd helped me through my drought. A fifty-pack of bud. To rest easy. With what was left of the money, I'd pay the internet bill and buy a couple of things we needed around the house. I didn't care about being broke, the good thing about working days and going to school at night is that you don't got time to want to spend money.

A junkie sold me a SuperVia card for two reals. Always a tricky transaction, buying that kind of thing from a crackhead, but he kept hanging around where I was working, and I wasn't going to move elsewhere on account of two reals. He assured me it had two train rides on it, which made going on the mission easier. It seemed like everything was conspiring in my favor. I even gave up on going to school that day, soon as I arrived on the hill I'd go straight to Cantão terrace, smoke some sick kush, soak up the view.

I don't usually take the train and had forgotten how, after five p.m., it's hell on earth. When I got there it was already full, with nowhere to sit and plenty of folks standing, though at least you could still breathe. Little by little, more people got on and the space around us quickly evaporated. The train doors would close, I'd feel relieved no one else was getting on, then the doors would open again, and people just kept piling in. Some grumbled at the delays in leaving the station, but most folks just kept their heads down, trying to guard their spot.

The train pulled out, hawkers trying their luck touted their wares, their legs planted in the space they'd conquered for themselves; it was impossible to walk in there, more so if you were carrying a Styrofoam container or a bunch of candy slung on a pole. I kept thinking about how I'd get to the door if the carriage didn't empty out before we reached my stop. Since it wasn't far from Central, I knew only a handful of people would get off before I reached my destination. What I hadn't pictured was that even more bodies could possibly get on when we pulled into São Cristóvão. Folks grumbled, said they should take the next train, there wasn't any room. The new passengers forced their way in through the doors, the people inside shoved them out. My body was swaying, even though I wasn't making a single movement when, from one moment to the next, everyone slotted into place, the doors closed, we continued on our way.

The rain started as we pulled into Maracanã Station. I hadn't put much faith in the clouds being powerful enough

to bring down water, but that's what happened. I thought of
how, sometimes, one person's perrengue can be another's joy.
My mind went to those two kids I'd met at Campo de San-
tana that time I'd gone searching for a joint on my lunch
break. The two of them were from Fallet, inseparable, like
Laurel and Hardy, except they were both so skinny it sometimes seemed they'd break at the slightest breeze. They always worked based on need: if it was hot, they sold water; if
it was raining, they sold umbrellas. The day I met them,
the guy who usually slung up that way was nowhere in sight,
word on the street was he might have been bagged. I was
pissed I'd have to spend the rest of the day straight, and the
two kids ended up throwing some bud my way, I don't even
know how we started talking. All I remember is that half-
way through the joint, lightning started flashing and the
wind kicked up. The two boys ran off:

"Rain! Told ya it'd come down today, I told ya!"

I yelled after them:

"Hey, your joint!"

They responded:

"Umbrellas are five, jumbos ten!"

And off they went to make some dough. I chuckled at
the scene, smoking my j under a tree, watching the rain fall.

By the time we reached Triagem, I was itching to get near
the door. A near impossible mission. I'd try to squeeze by, say
excuse me, no use. I'd try to force my way through, but the
bodies stiffened against mine. Someone would whine that I'd
stepped on their foot, I'd turn back, consider other avenues.
When the train stopped at Jacarezinho, I still wasn't as close
to the door as I would've liked, so I elbowed my way there,
bulldozing anyone in front of me, shielded by the fact that

I wouldn't be in the carriage to take any lip about my attitude.

I got out, looked up at the sky, the rain had let up, though it'd come down hard enough to muddy up the station's floor. I walked through the high-wheel exit; the vibe was weird. Those who are apprised know that on Fry-day Jacaré turns into Paris. At least for the junkies streaming in from all over the city. The favela wasn't deserted, but there were far fewer people than I'd imagined. I was kinda pissed. If there was a raid going down, I'd have to go over to Manguinhos.

There was a time when Jacaré bud was so hot, like fucking sizzling, that folks would queue up at the boca to get their hands on some. This one time, there I was bent over picking at some bud from a five-real bundle, when I looked to the side and there's Amaral, a buddy from the hill who works as a mototaxi driver. It was hilarious—never thought I'd bump into anyone from the hill in the favela, much less a dude terrified of stepping onto another faction's turf. We shot the breeze on the train tracks and fired one up in honor of our encounter. Only reason I didn't catch a ride on his bike was he only had one helmet and everybody knows it's rough carrying drugs across town when you're in the wrong.

I thought it was weird that there weren't any kids blazing on the street, which is the thing you most see when you walk into a favela. The bud's so copious here that looking down at the ground you'll find blunt ends big as your thumb. Which just didn't happen in places where the cost of weed was steeper, like in Vidigal, where folks smoke until their fingers and lips start to singe. Another strange thing was that no crackheads had rolled up to me when I'd walked out of the station. Usually they waste no time. They always want something from you, first they want some bud to mix with their crack so they can roll themselves a zirrê, then when you say no, they ask for a cigarette, a skin, a coin so they can buy some Guaravita. It's rough.

I walked to the boca. Nobody there. The tables and parasols were still out, but no trade in sight. I looked around, no cops, no caveirões rolling by, folks were walking along the street, taking it easy. I was straight-up confused: if the boca was deserted, how could everything be so quiet? I walked over to another boca I knew about up the way. A kid ran past me, must've been about twelve years old.

"What d'you need? Weed?"

"Yeah. Where everybody at?"

"They hiding! Tell me what you need."

"Gimme a bundle of fifty."

"We only got tens, take five, c'mon!"

I handed him the cash, and two seconds later, the kid had vanished into the back alleys.

I lit a cigarette and looked around me. The whole situation had me spooked. I'd come to Jacarezinho plenty of times before with slugs flying solid, but all you had to do then was walk over to Manguinhos or take the bus to another favela from Avenida Suburbana so the trip wasn't wasted. But I'd never seen it like that, it felt like shots might start whizzing past any minute now, with me smack in the middle of the cross fire, standing there like bait, not knowing which way to run, in a favela that's not even my own.

The kid came by with the weed. It wasn't as richly served as usual, but, even so, better than the stuff you could get on the hill. I asked him:

"Is it busted here, mano?"

He said:

"Cops came through earlier, but they gone now. Shots fired, but everybody's cleared out. It's cool, take it easy."

I spread the bud across several pockets then walked back to the station. Stopped at a bar to buy skins. If the SuperVia hadn't arrived, I'd fire one up by the tracks while I waited for the train. I took the skins, handed the woman the cash. She said something I didn't catch, I thanked her and walked off. I'd spend the other ride on my card instead of jumping the turnstile. I didn't wanna jump and get my clothes all mucked up with mud 'cause cops at Central might catch on. As I come up to the station entrance, that's when I understand what the lady had tried to tell me: "Watch out for the five-o!"

The MP pointed his gun at my face. It wasn't the first and wouldn't be the last time somebody pointed a weapon at me.

"Hands above your head," he said.

I raised them, another MP went and put his hand on my waist, checking if I was strapped. The .40 staring straight at me.

"He's clean," the other guy said.

"You got drugs on you?"

I realized I was surrounded by four military cops.

"Yes, I do, officer. Five bundles of ten."

I took them out of my pocket one by one and handed them over to the blue blood.

"Where do you live?"

"Leblon," I said. And seeing he didn't believe me, I added: "My dad's the doorman of a building there."

In these kinds of situations, it's always best to say you live down on the blacktop, especially if you're caught on another faction's turf. 'Cause if the cops catch on, you better be ready to face a mad fury.

"What else you got in that bag?"

All I had was a jacket, a book, and, inside the book, one hundred reals, the rest of my pay. The pig's eyes glittered when he caught sight of the dough, but he kept a straight face, placed it in my hand, and told me to hold on to the cash.

"I gotta say, kid, you look like a smart guy. So tell me, what's the parley?"

"Ain't no parley. I've lost the weed, you can take it. I need the money to pay the electric."

"What do you mean nothing? You come all the way down here, give us all this trouble, and you're telling me we ain't gonna come to an agreement?"

"That's right. If you want, you can take me down to the station. I'll sign whatever I gotta sign, but I'm taking that money home."

"You sure you wanna go down to the station with ten bundles of weed?"

"I only handed you five."

"How many you got there, captain?"

And the captain, who was holding a 12-gauge, answered: "Ten!"

That's when I noticed none of them were wearing IDs on their uniforms. I couldn't believe they were trying to fucking frame me, making me take the rap for drug trafficking. Also, no one could guarantee that, if I left with them, I'd even end up at the station. They could just make me disappear and keep the scratch. I knew I was gonna lose out, but I couldn't believe it. I'd spent the whole week thinking about that money, planning what I'd do with it, it was like we were pals. I tried one last time:

"I need that money. It's for my electricity bills, I swear, officer."

"Son, when a brother gets caught, he forgets his bills. Everybody knows the deal. Even the old-timers know that's how things roll. You lost, you lose, kid."

By that point, I'd come to the realization that the internet bill was going to have to wait and the vibe at home would be tense for another week; I tried to at least save some of the grass:

"Easy, y'all can take the scratch. But let me keep the weed."

The way things were going, I didn't think he'd accept any conditions I put down. His response took me by surprise:

"Sure, I'll put it in your backpack."

I made to place the hundred in the cop's hand, he said:

"You crazy, kid. Put your hand here, inside the pack. There you go. Leave the bill in there and I'll take it off you."

I left the bill, he handed me the pack.

"The weed in here?"

"Of course. Do I look like the kind of guy who'd double-talk you?"

I opened the bag, checked for the bud, right there in front of them. They kept watching me, the weed was there. I closed the backpack. Then I remembered something:

"That's all the cash I had, I need money to pay for a ticket from Central to Leblon."

The cop came up to me, handed me two ten-real notes, and walked off with his partners. I was so pissed that, if I could, I would've killed the four of them right then and there, without blinking. A slow, painful death, the kind every pig deserves. I walked to the station, reached the turnstile, swiped my card: "Insufficient fare." Motherfucker! There are days when everything's outta whack, when your luck just blows. I walked to the middle of the station, jumped over as usual, got my shirt all covered in mud, but I didn't care anymore. At the station, folks asked me:

"What happened with those five-o up the way, were you dirty?"

"Five bundles of ten."

"They take it all?"

"Hell no. I had a hundred reais on me for the electric, they took every last fucking cent! But I said to them: 'Nah, you gotta at least leave me the drugs.' And they did."

"Shit, son, those motherfuckers are messed up!"

Lots of folks at the station got all worked up about my story, everyone had something to say, cursing out those pigs. I'd stopped talking and busied myself skinning up, blood in my eyes. Whenever I thought I was done, I'd look down at my hand, figure it wasn't enough, throw in a bit more, keep on rolling . . . As I thought of all the perrengues I'd ever gotten into with the cops, I felt this fierce weight on my chest. When I lit the blunt, I realized what I'd rolled was more like a cigar, a bazooka big as the arm of Judas, or the finger of God. I kept on smoking and the bud was crisp, rich. But as I breathed in that smoke, it rode into my lungs thick with such hatred, sadness, and hopelessness that I couldn't help thinking that those sons of bitches should've just taken the goddamned weed with them, too.

# THE CROSSING

"Ain't gonna tell you twice: get that motherfucking corpse outta my sight. If anybody misses that fool and lands me with another conviction, *you'll* be the one in the ditch, motherfucker! Now go, get outta my face, 'cause ain't nothing worse in this world than a stupid-ass thug."

It's fucked up to hear that kind of talk from the boss, enough to make anyone shit their pants. Beto had never spoken to him before, and this is how it went down, his ass handed to him in front of everyone on the hill.

Beto hadn't fired his gun once since he'd started dealing in the bocas, more than a year ago now. That shit messed with his head, standing around holding a goddamn machine gun he never got to use. Almost like the fucking thing was just for show. Sometimes, still buzzing from a baile funk, he'd pretend to stake out alleys, all wild-eyed, pointing his piece at shit that wasn't there. There were loads of others like him, young kids who'd started working bocas when the hill was dead quiet, the brass scared off and no rival crews even thinking about invading. It wasn't that Beto wanted to put his neck on the line, he often sat around eyeing his machine gun and his pistol, picturing what would happen if the BOPE suddenly showed up and started coming down on them. All it took was a straight shot and tchau, you're toast, that's the truth of it. Way things were going now though, no way was he ever gonna win the crew's respect, and that got him all worked up. Everybody knows if a thug's gonna earn their stripes, it's in combat, the moment they prove their heart pumps cold. Now he's gone and got himself into the fix of figuring out how to dump the corpse.

And all 'cause dude made the other faction's sign after taking his eight-ball. If Beto'd known shit would hit the fan, he would've just slapped the guy around a bit, or maybe even let the fool run. But nah, he'd pumped the son of a bitch full of lead instead. The moment he opened fire, he kind of knew he'd fucked up—too late, though. Now this. What's worse, looking at the dead fool now, all that hate he'd felt, the rush and the adrenaline, were gone, and kid was just God's son again, some mama's child.

It was gonna be a bitch getting hold of a car to take him across to the landfill. Folks knew what'd gone down, and it seemed to him he'd already been pegged as a favela fuckup. Then there was the risk for the guy who owned the car, if it was registered, all that stuff. No way around it, though; not like he could walk the body out or hitch it a ride on a moto-taxi. Beto kept thinking: "Been working bocas for over a year now and never once bought myself nothing. No TV set, no PlayStation neither. It's rough being a broke-ass thug. Time when this shit made you rich is long gone. Back when I was a kid, I was always seeing guys riding motorbikes and buying imported cars off dudes who swiped them off the blacktop.

Now it's twelve-hour shifts, seven days a week. And next thing you know, you're broke, eating ready-made meals bought on credit. Fuck that noise!"

He went around asking guys he used to sell to for a loan, but nobody wanted to get mixed up in his mess. Some made up excuses, others just spat: "You fucked up, kid. Gotta face the music." Beto was pissed; when fool wants a solid 'cause he fresh out of dope, when he's mid-funk and wants a huff, when he asks to hold your gun 'cause he's hitting on a babe, then you tight. But when *you* need a hand, this all they got for you? He couldn't stop thinking about the body stashed in his shack. The hot, bright sun makes everything smell ripe—sewage, trash, death. If the stiff started stinking before he got it out, the stench would be hell to clean up.

But what really hacked Beto off was he just couldn't figure what the boss's deal was. Dude had a rap sheet longer than his arm, and he feeds him that bullshit line? Would've been nothing to just stash the fool in the woods. Cops don't come looking for drugs, you think they gonna come looking for a junkie? Please. Nothing he could do, though, you gotta respect the hierarchy, he'd learned that much as a kid.

He bought a Chevette to pay off later. Dealer in the store guaranteed it'd make it to the landfill. Beto was becoming more and more desperate. He knew the car was the classic ride for pigs to pull over. Wrong-looking, no registration, busted headlights—cops would roll up thirsting for breakfast. And if they peeped the body, that was it, they'd try and squeeze him for the month's groceries, too, and Christmas presents, as if he was flush with spare dough to hand over to the brass. At first, he thought he'd soft-pedal the body over in the morning. But then he convinced himself that if a cop caught him in that car at the crack of dawn, it'd take a miracle not to be pulled over. Trick was to leave that same afternoon, and pray God protect him on his crossing. It'd been a while since Beto had taken the wheel, on the hill he only ever went on motorbike. But he'd have to face this mess himself, no way he'd find a driver up for the mission.

Dead guy was all bunched up in the trunk of the rolling Chevette. "Wonder what his name is," Beto thought. No ID on him, no cell phone, no nothing. "Wonder if a dude like him's got a family. Hope not," he then thought. Which made him think about his own ma, of how they started growing apart once he got to his teens, of how things started changing when he stopped going to mass and started smoking weed on the street, about how they'd argued—she'd always dreamed her son would be a priest. For the first time that day, he considered how his old lady would take it when the news finally reached her. Rough enough having your kid working bocas, but a murderer to boot, goddamn, no way would the church sisters let that one go. Those old biddies are rough, they know more about other folks' lives than they do the Bible.

The landfill wasn't far, but he was so strung out in that Chevette that after thirty minutes at the wheel, he couldn't handle the pressure anymore. His whole body ached, like he'd just taken a thrashing. Suddenly, the worst possible thing happened: the car died. Beto looked around him, quickly clocked where he was: militia turf. "Now shit's well and truly fucked," he thought. Cashless, he knew the only parley with these guys was bullets. No breed worse in this world to get into shit with than the militia—not only are they rotten to the bone, they under police protection, too. He stayed put, trying to think up a solution. He felt he was being watched. A group of old-timers was playing pool and drinking beer at a bar across the street. One of them must be militia, just had to be.

No way around it, three of the old-timers crossed the street toward the Chevette. Two of them were shirtless and Beto could tell they weren't strapped. Except the only one with a shirt had a militia look about him, Beto could even see his gun bulging at his hip. He pictured how he'd drop, if they'd come down on him right there and leave a mess for someone else to clean up, if they'd take him to some other place or get a single shot to the head, or if they'd decide not to skimp on bullets to riddle his body. Maybe if he told them the dead guy was a junkie piece of shit, they'd go easy on him, he thought, those motherfuckers hate junkies. Trouble was having to explain all those bullet holes—and what's he doing with a goddamn machine gun, anyway? Wouldn't be long before they clocked that Beto was working at the boca, and then, meu amigo, it'd be talk of all kinds of torture if the dough didn't show. And it wouldn't. He was scorched on the hill now, no point trying. Fools wouldn't think twice before ordering him dead, 'cause a fuckup's place is six feet under. His mind went to his ma again, to her hugs, her eyes, her voice. He was so sure he was done for, he even started thinking about God.

The Chevette's exhaust pipe popped like a gunshot, but he was free and easy on the road. He couldn't believe those old-timers had helped him push the car. He'd lent a hand in that kind of situation before, even when he didn't know the driver. But he never considered somebody'd return the favor, and on one of the worst days of his life. "Saving others, you save yourself, too," he thought. It was starting to feel like things would turn out all right, they had to. He was a rookie to this shit, never fucked up before, saw no reason he should be blackballed forever.

That's when he reached the landfill. It was getting dark and folks were still milling around rifling for junk, though none wanting to peep anything they shouldn't. Which is why he pulled out the body from inside the trunk, dead easy, rolled up in that black trash bag. Fool was heavy as fuck, considering he was a junkie and Batsuit-thin when he was sent to a better place. If he'd dumped the kid in the bushes, he would've covered him in a blanket of tires, perfumed him with petrol, and set fire to the sorry fool. But it was too risky here, the flames could set off licking everything in sight, somebody might see what he'd done and say something. There's always someone watching. That he'd learned on the hill, where fuckups always drop, one time or another. He dumped the body right there, figured the vultures would end it before anyone came looking.

Now to head home and try and win back the boca boys' trust. Show them shit had flown but it was all in the past now, nobody's perfect, and any fool can lose his head from one moment to the next. Beto couldn't decide if he should show his face for the next shift or wait till the dust settled before rolling up on the quiet. He hated all this shit. It was like a nightmare, the kind you never woke up from.

Everything went to pieces when he got to the hill. He was on his way to take his shift, thinking he best show himself sooner than later so fools wouldn't start talking crap about what'd gone down. He glanced at the alleys, at folks on the street, the cachaça-drinking drunks, the stoners, the believers, the girls, the workers heading home. Everything seemed different, as if, back from his mission, he was seeing the hill for the first time. It was straight-up wild. He got to the boca, everybody taking it easy, smoking up, shooting the shit. One pusher bellowed, "Come get your kush!" Another: "Ten-real cola, you snort you tweak, ten-real cola, bring your sniffers!" So far, business as usual. But when they spotted Beto, the boca fell quiet. He knew at once, from the looks on all their faces, that there'd be no getting past anything. It ain't pretty going down as a favela fuckup. Without a wake or a tribute. He knew the lieutenant had it in for him, that he was just waiting for the right time to fuck with his life. If anybody, he'd be the one to pull the trigger, Beto was sure of it. But, instead of a bullet, what he got was a warning to clear out; don't bother stopping at your crib or kissing anybody goodbye 'cause the hill's no place for a hotheaded kid who can't handle the burden of carrying a piece.

That shit's messed up, no kid thinks he'll have to quit the place he was born and raised, with folks saying he'd cut and run on account of wasting. Beto turned right around and left; if they shot him in the back, fuck it, what difference did it make. No idea where he was gonna sleep. Nobody came at him. His sentence really was to bolt, and it stung like a bullet. He loved and hated that hill like nobody could ever understand or explain. He looked at those alleyways and remembered some things from way back when: Cosmas Day, always scampering up and down, playing with Bob

Teco, sling-shooting rats. He remembered the dreams he dreamed as a kid, what he used to think his life would be like, back then he never thought he'd be selling drugs. He'd wanted to become a soccer player, an airplane pilot, an IT tech. Now, as he heads down the slopes and off the hill, all he can think about is how everything's going to be so, so different.

## A NOTE ABOUT THE AUTHOR

Geovani Martins was born in 1991 in Rio de Janeiro, Brazil. He grew up with his mother in the Rio neighborhood of Vidigal. He supported his writing by working as a sandwich-board man and selling drinks on the beach, and was discovered during creative writing workshops at FLUP, the literary festival of the Rio favelas. *The Sun on My Head* is his first book.

## A NOTE ABOUT THE TRANSLATOR

Julia Sanches translates from the Portuguese, Spanish, French, and Catalan. She has translated works by Susana Moreira Marques, Noemi Jaffe, Daniel Galera, Claudia Hernández, and Liliana Colanzi, among others. Her work has also appeared in *Two Lines*, *Granta*, *Tin House*, *Words Without Borders*, and *Electric Literature*. She is a founding member of the Cedilla & Co. translators' collective, and lives in Providence, Rhode Island.